DEATH MATCH

Suddenly Waite was on top of him. His huge thumbs were crushing Dan's windpipe. Thinking fast, Dan reached up and closed his fingers on the big man's nose, twisting it violently. When he felt the cartilage snap, he knew the nose was broken. For a moment Waite lost his balance, and Dan slipped out from under him. Waite groped his way to his feet, blood bubbling from his nostrils. Dan didn't give the man time to fortify himself. He closed in, anger burning in his veins like raw whisky. . . .

Other Exciting Westerns by Morgan Hill

DEAD MAN'S NOOSE
TWIN COLTS

Other Blazing Western Adventures from Dell Books

WILSON'S LUCK Giles Tippette

THE HAVENS RAID Greg Hunt

GUNLOCK Wayne D. Overholser

FOXX! Zack Tyler

WEST OF RIMROCK Wayne D. Overholser

BLACK HATS David Case

THE QUICK AND THE DEADLY

MORGAN HILL

A DELL BOOK

Published by
Dell Publishing Co., Inc.
1 Dag Hammarskjold Plaza
New York, New York 10017

Copyright © 1981 by Morgan Hill

All rights reserved. No part of this book may be reproduced or transmitted in any form or by any means, electronic or mechanical, including photocopying, recording or by any information storage and retrieval system, without the written permission of the Publisher except where permitted by law.

Dell ® TM 681510, Dell Publishing Co., Inc.

ISBN: 0-440-17173-3

Printed in the United States of America
First printing—February 1981

CHAPTER ONE

Dan Colt spurred the black gelding when he heard the gunfire just over the rim of the shallow canyon to his left. Peering down agaist the sharp rays of the lowering sun, he saw five riders in pursuit of the Wells Fargo stage. The stage had left Durango, heading north, about half an hour before Dan had ridden out. Because of the curves in the road for the first ten miles he had cut across country in a straight line, intending to drop out of the high ridge country, back onto the road.

The team was at a full gallop. The stagecoach bobbed and weaved at the excessive speed, careening dangerously on the winding curves. Colt could see a man firing at the riders from inside the coach as the road bottomed out and became a steep climb. First would appear the white puffs of smoke from the muzzles, followed by the delayed sound of the guns, traveling to his ears.

Just before the coach and its pursuers passed from his view, Dan saw the shotgunner buckle, drop his gun, and lean over the side.

The big black thundered down the side of the mountain, dodging trees and boulders. Once again Colt could see the coach as it labored up the steep grade. The shotgunner had disappeared, and the driver was firing his pistol wildly at the riders. The man was still firing from the inside.

When the coach passed from sight again, the tall

blond man on the black saw a wide open clearing ahead, where he could climb the grade parallel to the road and ride ahead of the coach.

The wind whistled in his ears as he topped the ridge and rode about halfway down the next grade. In one smooth move he pulled his Winchester from the boot and hit the ground with both feet. Dodging behind a boulder, he peered back up the road. The stagecoach was just coming over the crest. The way it was bobbing and weaving, Dan did not wonder that the man firing from inside was unable to hit his pursuers. One rider was out in front. Two others flanked the coach, slightly to the rear. The other two followed.

Levering a shell into the chamber, he drew a bead on the lead rider, led him a fraction, and squeezed the trigger. The man peeled off his horse sideways and fell directly in front of the careening stage. The right front and back wheels ran over him. By this time Colt had squeezed off another shot and dropped another rider.

The others were pulling back and scattering to Dan's side of the road. On the opposite side was a sheer drop of over five hundred feet. Dan leveled and fired on the last rider to leave the road. The man fell hard to the ground and lay motionless.

A popping noise, sounding like lightning-split timber, met Dan's ears as the stage passed him at full speed. One of the left-side wheels dropped off just as the coach met a sharp curve. The coach lurched to the left as the axle hit the rocky road. Dan saw the driver leap in the opposite direction as the off-balance team and stagecoach went over the edge. One of the horses gave a death scream.

Checking up the road for sight of the other two riders, Dan saw nothing. He ran across the road in time to see the stagecoach turn upside down in midair while the four horses became a scrambled mass of pawing legs and flailing hoofs. Several pine trees were sheared and splintered with the impact. Horses and stagecoach came to a sudden stop in a muddled heap. One wheel broke loose and rolled around in a wide circle, slammed against a boulder, and fell flat. The only movement as the dust cleared was the spinning of a remaining wheel, which was positioned horizontally above the rough canyon bottom.

The sun had already dropped behind the tall peaks to the west. Dan Colt was sure that whoever was in the stagecoach was undoubtedly dead. Wheeling from the edge of the cliff, he sprinted down the road to the fallen driver. The man was sprawled face down on the side of the road. His head was split wide open. He had hit the ground hard, his head taking the full impact on a large jagged rock. Dan dragged his body off the road.

With the sun down the mid-April mountain air grew cold quickly. Dan walked to his horse and pulled his Mackinaw from under the bedroll.

Daylight was fading as he rode the black gelding south over the steep incline, looking for the shotgunner. He loped the big horse down the other side, searching for the place where he had seen the man buckle and start to fall. As he neared the spot, a large timber wolf stood over the man, licking the blood around the shoulder wound. Hearing the approach of the hoofbeats, it raised its head, licking the blood from its chops.

Dan pulled the gelding to a halt about fifteen yards from where the wolf stood. The huge animal crouched low and bared its fangs in defiance of the horse and rider.

"Go on, boy," said Dan with a firm voice. "I don't want to harm you." The horse was trembling beneath him. It was prancing sideways in spite of Dan Colt's firm tug on the reins.

Slowly the tall man slid the Winchester from the boot. A deep growl came from the throat of the wolf. The horse whinnied in fear, its eyes wild.

Then the wolf came. Dan brought the rifle to bear and fired, but the gelding reared to meet the charging beast. The shot went wild. As the big wolf met the horse with a powerful impact, horse and rider fell over backward. Dan managed to fall free of the big black. He rolled to one side and looked toward the wolf. Agile and lithe, the angry animal quickly found its balance and lunged for the man. The horse, now on its feet, reared and pawed the air with a shrill cry.

Dan saw the wolf coming and realized he had dropped the rifle. The beast was on him before he could move. Instinctively he raised his left arm and felt the sharp fangs pierce the heavy Mackinaw. He tried to roll himself free, and in the struggle he felt a clawed foot rake his face. Again he lifted his left arm as the bared fangs aimed for his face. The angry beast was standing spread-legged over him.

The wolf was shaking its head and snapping fiercely, trying to get at Dan's throat. Swinging his left elbow hard at the animal's mouth, he reached down with his right hand and slipped the Colt .45 from its holster. Pressing the muzzle against the wolf's belly, he fired.

The wolf leaped backward with a wild yelp of pain, staggered slightly, and lunged for Dan again. The slight stagger gave the bleeding man time to aim the pistol and fire again. The bullet caught the animal square between the eyes. Its legs buckled and it dropped dead in its tracks.

Dan gathered his legs under him and slowly rose to his feet. The horse blew and pawed at the dirt with both hoofs. Wiping blood from his left eye, the tall man staggered in the gathering darkness toward the fallen shotgun rider.

Dropping to one knee, he heard the wounded

man's labored breathing. Apparently the wolf had just found him as Dan had arrived on the scene.

The bullet had struck him in the shoulder from behind. He had fallen from the speeding vehicle and struck his head on the ground. He was still unconscious. The blood was seeping through the shotgunner's denim jacket, but as far as Dan could tell, he was not bleeding profusely. Still, he was going to need attention soon, or he would bleed to death.

Wiping the trickle of blood from his left eye again, Dan mounted the black and rode over the grade to where he had seen the outlaws' horses grazing near the bodies of their riders. Bringing the black alongside a blaze-faced bay mare, he reached over and swung the reins over the horse's head. There was a moment of difficulty, as the two animals insisted on rubbing noses.

Dan felt the effect of his battle with the wolf as he hoisted the unconscious man onto the bay's saddle. The shotgunner was not a large man, but it was all Dan's weakened arms and unstable legs could do to get him on the horse. He laid him chest down over the saddle and, using the man's belt, fastened him to the pommel.

Once again heading north, Dan followed the road, leading the bay. It was totally dark now, and there was no moon. The stars twinkled in the heavens as Dan searched the darkness ahead for some speck of light.

As the road wound downward toward a dark valley, he noticed that the bleeding above his eye had stopped. Dan wondered if the claw marks would leave scars. Slowly the horses felt their way along the road. From time to time Dan drew the bay alongside to check the shotgunner.

About an hour had passed when a faint gleam of light caught Dan's eye. Off to his left, through the thick forest, he could make out light shining through two windows. Veering off the road, he moved toward the welcome sight.

When he was within two hundred yards of the house, his ears picked up the sound of a gurgling stream. He soon approached it, wondering how deep it might be. Squinting against the darkness, he looked left, then right. To the right he saw what he assumed to be a flat log bridge. Urging the horses in that direction, he saw that his assumption was correct and took them over the bridge. The hoofs made a soft, hollow sound, then clopped again on the hard earth.

It was not until they approached the house and surrounding buildings that Dan became aware of the pain in his left arm. The wolf's fangs had penetrated the heavy coat and left the sleeve in shreds.

He pulled the horses to a stop about thirty feet from the back door. He started to lift his left hand to cup the side of his mouth. A bolt of pain shot all the way up his shoulder. Easing it back down, he shouted, "Hello the house!"

Instantly the lights inside faded and disappeared. All was quiet.

"Hello the house!" Dan shouted again.

"Get out of here right now!" a female voice answered back.

"I need—" Dan's words were cut short as a window flew open and a rifle barked. The bullet hummed past his ear.

"Hey, wait a minute!" Dan bellowed as he swung the horses in retreat.

The rifle roared again. "Get out of here, you dirty skunks!" the voice rasped from behind the gun. "You get off this property"—the gun belched orange flame again—"or I'll bury you in it!"

The rifle had the deep sound of a Sharps buffalo gun, and Dan Colt knew if she kept firing, one of the horses, the shotgunner, or he himself was going to get hit. One slug from the big gun would tear a mighty big hole.

"Wait a minute, ma'am!" he shouted at the top of his voice. "I'm a stranger in these parts, and I've got a wounded man here! He'll die if he doesn't get help!"

Silence.

"Ma'am!" Dan backed the horses a little further. The wind was picking up. A chill went through Dan's weary body. "Ma'am!"

Silence.

For a moment Dan wished for the moon. The darkness was so heavy he could feel it. Then he was glad for the darkness. If the woman behind the gun could see him, he would probably be dead.

"Hey, ma'am!"

"Right here." The voice came from behind him. Spinning his head, he could make out a small form, holding the rifle directly on him.

"You're not one of Mel Curry's men?" she asked.

"No, ma'am," Dan answered courteously. "A gang of men tried to hold up the Wells Fargo stage just before sundown. I rode up on it and managed to scatter the gang. Killed three of them. Stage went over a cliff. Driver's dead. I've got the shotgun rider here. He's shot up pretty bad."

The woman called past Dan toward the house. "Patty Ruth! Light a lantern and bring it out here." Keeping the muzzle squared on the big man on the gelding, she said, "Move over by the house, *slow*, mister. Make a fast move and it will be your last."

Cautiously Dan kneed the big black and headed toward the house. Light flickered in the rear window, went low, and then rose to a bright glow. Presently a small girl, Dan estimated she was seven or eight, emerged from the door. The lantern in her hand revealed a pretty face adorned with long dark hair.

"Hold the light still, Patty Ruth," the woman said

from behind the horses. "Now, mister, get off the horse real slow and put your face in the light."

Stiffly the tall man swung out of the saddle with the sound of creaking leather. The woman was circling the horses as Dan exposed his face in the yellow light. She eyed him closely, bringing her own face into view. There was no doubt that she was Patty Ruth's mother. Her face was just a grown-up version of the little girl's. Womanhood had only made it prettier.

"Bring the lantern over here, honey," said the mother, moving toward the bay. Studying the shotgunner closely, she turned to Dan. "We'd better get him inside. He looks bad. And you don't look so good yourself."

CHAPTER TWO

Slipping the wounded man from the saddle, Dan laid him over his shoulder and followed the two females into the house. His legs felt like boiled mush.

"Just put him down here on the sofa," the woman said, bracing the heavy Sharps against the wall. Stepping to the fireplace, she stirred the fire with a poker and placed a couple of logs in the flames. As she did so, she spoke over her shoulder. "Patty Ruth, get the other lantern out of the bedroom and tell Danny to come in here."

Placing the lantern on the table, Patty Ruth hurried into the dark room at the front of the house. Dan had found a butcher knife and was cutting away the shotgunner's shirt and jacket when the little girl entered the room carrying a lantern in one hand and leading a wide-eyed little boy with the other.

The boy broke away from his sister and ran to his mother. "It's all right, honey," she said, "these men won't hurt us. They're friends."

Dan took note that the boy was his namesake. He estimated him to be about five.

The pretty woman was lighting the second lantern. Dan studied her face for a moment. She was small; barely over five feet. Slender and delicate. He wondered where the husband was.

Pouring hot water into a shallow basin, she pulled a chair next to the sofa and placed the basin on it. Kneeling beside Dan, she examined the unconscious man. "That bullet is buried deep, but it will have to come out. Help me turn him over."

Dan complied. Standing up, he removed his gray Stetson and hung it on the back of a chair. Gingerly he took off the Mackinaw, wincing as the tattered sleeve came over the wounded forearm.

The woman looked up at him from her kneeling position. "How in the world—?"

"Wolf," Dan replied dryly. The blood had caked under the sleeve, and some of the fragments had clung to it. In removing the coat, Dan had unwittingly started it bleeding again.

"Let me—"

"We can tend to me later," he said as she started to rise. "Let's take care of him."

Dan held him down while the lady probed for the bullet. Her hands were steady, strong, and adept. Shortly she produced the bloody slug and called for Dan to hold extra hard as she poured whisky in the wound. The unconscious man jerked violently.

Within a quarter hour she had sutured the wound with sewing thread and had it bandaged firmly. "I believe he will live," she said to Dan with a warm smile. "He took an awful knock on the head. We'll have to bring him around by morning and get some liquid in him. He lost a lot of blood."

Looking up into the tall man's face, she said, "Now you sit down over here by the table and let me work on you."

Procuring a fresh basin of hot water, she dipped in a clean cloth and began cleansing the wounded arm. "The bites aren't deep," she said assuringly. "Your heavy coat took most of the damage."

Having washed it thoroughly, she reached for the whisky bottle. Dan's eyes widened. "Now don't tell me a big six-foot-four-inch bruiser like you is going to be a scairdy cat."

"I'm only six-three," he answered, swallowing hard.

The whisky burned like blue blazes, but Dan bit down hard and took it without a vocal outburst. Applying a strong-smelling salve, she bandaged the wounded area.

Turning her attention to his clawed face, she pushed back his matted blond locks and lifted the lantern to get a close look. Dan Colt had not been this close to a woman since his wife had died. Nervously he tried to think of something to say.

"Think it'll leave scars?" he asked cautiously.

"I don't think so. Probably be marked till the red goes away after the scabs come off."

After she had daubed the scratches with whisky, she said, "Now you just sit there and rest while I put the children to bed." Standing up, she took the children by their hands. "Tell Mr.— Goodness! I haven't asked your name."

"Dan Colt, ma'am," the blond man said quietly.

"I'm sorry," she said with a slight blush. "I'm Lily Dolan. This is Patty Ruth. This is Danny." Looking at the boy, she said, "Danny, this man has your name."

Danny managed a weak smile. "Yes, ma'am."

"Tell Mr. Colt good night, children."

The children complied and were escorted to the bedroom. Dan looked around the room. It was clean and well kept. His eyes fell on a mirror above a small table bearing a wash basin and shaving cup. A razor strap hung next to the mirror. *Husband must be on a trip somewhere*, he told himself.

Dan walked to the mirror and examined his face. The claw marks started just below the hairline on the left side of his forehead, dropped toward his eye, then curved sharply toward his temple. There was a deep gouge over the cheekbone. He felt around the eye lightly with his fingertips. *Lucky*, he thought. *Could have lost the eye.*

He stepped back from the mirror and looked at his

bandaged forearm. Flexing his fingers, he wondered if the wounds would affect his draw. Facing the mirror, he drew the Colt .45 in the left holster. Dropping it back in the holster, he repeated the action several times.

"Got anyone particular in mind?" Lily asked from behind.

Dan's face flushed as he spun around. "Not at the moment. Just wanted to be sure about the left hand."

"And?"

"Seems all right. A little pain, but I don't think it'll slow me down."

"I haven't seen a badge," she said soberly, "so I assume you are a gunfighter of some sort. You're not an outlaw, or you wouldn't have helped Wells Fargo today."

"I used to be a gunslinger. Hired out as bodyguard. That sort of thing. Did some bounty hunting."

"Where are you from, Mr. Colt?" she asked, feeling the brow of the unconscious man on the sofa.

"All over, ma'am," Dan said, swinging his right hand in a wide arc. "Let's don't talk about me. What about you . . . and these kids here . . . all alone? Who's this Mel Curry you were ready to blow to kingdom come?"

Lily's pretty brow furrowed. She bit her lower lip, and Dan saw fear fill her brown eyes. "Tom—that's my husband—left here three days ago, Mr. Colt, to get help from the marshal at Welcome."

"Welcome?"

"Yes. Town about twelve miles north of here."

"You mean there's a town called *Welcome, Colorado?*" Dan asked, twisting his face in unbelief.

"Uh-huh. It's right on the road between here and Ouray."

"I must've missed it when I was through here before," Dan observed, shaking his head. "I was tracking some killers from Wyoming. Sometimes they avoided the road. Anyway, go ahead."

Lily walked to the cupboard. "Let me fix you some supper while I tell you about it."

Dan lifted his hands in protest. "Aw, ma'am, you don't need to—"

"Aren't you hungry?" Lily butted in.

"Hadn't thought about it till you brought it up. Guess I am . . . a little," said the tall man shyly. Standing up, he walked to the fireplace and tossed in a couple of logs. Satisfied they would burn all right, he made his way to the table and sat down.

Lily stoked the fire in the stove and busied herself as she resumed the conversation. "Melvin Curry has a large ranch just west of here, which runs adjacent to our property. About six months ago he decided his ranch wasn't big enough, so he set his sights on our hundred and eighty-five acres. The greedy cur wants it especially because of the river that runs through here.

"Tom let him know right off that our place was not for sale. Curry had offered a ridiculously low price to begin with. Then he came back and doubled it."

Dan watched the back of her dark head and thought of Mary. A pang of sorrow and loneliness washed over him.

"Tom told him the place was not for sale at any price." She laid a clean plate and eating utensils before Dan. "Coffee will be hot in a minute," she said with a smile.

"I take it Curry has given you trouble," Dan said, rubbing his thick blond mustache.

"To put it mildly," Lily replied, her lips pulling in a thin line. "Four of them, including Curry, came here and beat Tom badly and threatened to work on the children and me next if Tom didn't sell."

Dan's eyes widened. He arched his eyebrows and made a low whistle.

"That was a week ago today. As soon as Tom was able, he saddled up and rode for Welcome . . ." Her words trailed off, and Dan saw tears in her eyes.

"Three days is a mighty long time, ma'am. Has anyone gone looking for him?" Dan asked with a note of concern.

"Neighbor from four miles north of here came by to see Tom yesterday morning. Bill Rice. Tom was already overdue, so Bill said he would ride to Welcome and look for him. When Bill didn't return by sundown yesterday, I went to the shed where we keep the buckboard. I was going to drive over to the Rice ranch. The buckboard was gone. So were all the horses." Lily's lip was quivering as she fought back the tears.

"Curry?"

"I'm sure of it," she answered, turning her back and using a corner of her apron to dry the tears. Dan scraped his chair back and stood up. Stepping up behind her, he squeezed both shoulders. Lily spun around and buried her face in his chest. She broke into heavy sobs.

"Mr. Colt . . . I'm so scared. Something's happened to Tom. I'm afraid to take the children away from the house on foot. If Curry or his men catch us out in the open—"

"First thing in the morning, ma'am, I've got to ride back and check on that busted up stagecoach. There was at least one passenger. Shouldn't take me long. If Tom isn't back by then, I'll ride to Welcome for you."

"But you may be on your way somewhere. I can't ask you to—"

"You didn't ask me. I volunteered," Dan said softly.

Lily was in control of herself again. She motioned for Dan to sit down and poured him a steaming cup of black coffee. Suddenly he jumped up and headed for the door.

"What is it?" she asked following.

"My horse," he answered as he stepped out in the dark. "Don't want Curry's bunch stealing him!"

Lily waited in the doorway as Dan heaved a sigh of relief. "They're both here," he called from the darkness. Leading the horses into the shaft of light that spilled through the open door, he said, "As soon as I get some food in me, I'll take them to the barn and bed down with them for the night."

Lily rubbed her arms as the chill of the night air touched her body. Tying both horses to one of the four-by-fours which supported the porch roof, Dan walked back into the house and closed the door. As Lily loaded his plate with food, he bent over the unconscious shotgunner. "Sure hope he comes out of it by morning," he said, returning to the table.

The food was delicious. Dan ate like a starving beast.

As Lily washed the dishes, Dan lingered over a fourth cup of coffee. He knew she was eaten up with worry over her husband. He was trying to think of something to say when she sat down on the opposite side of the table and set her dark eyes on him. "Do you have a wife waiting at home, Mr. Colt?"

A cold shaft of ice stabbed his heart. He tried to disguise the inward pain by holding his face expressionless, but Lily read his eyes. "Oh, I'm sorry. I shouldn't have—"

Dan managed an arduous smile. "No, please. Don't feel bad, Mrs. Dolan. My wife is dead. She was murdered by three drifters while I was away from home."

Lily's mouth went firm. "Were they caught? Did the law—"

"Judge Colt took care of it for two of them," Dan said blandly, "down in Holbrook, Arizona."

"Judge Colt? Is he a relative of yours?"

"No," said Dan, a furtive grin touching his lips, "the name is only a coincidence. But he's my closest friend." Slowly he slipped one of the .45s from its holster. Holding it loosely in his palm, he said, "Judge Colt, I want you to meet Mrs. Dolan."

Lily dipped her chin. "Oh." She cleared her throat. "And the third one?"

"Caught him over in New Mexico. Near Silver City. Fists. I had a lot of anger stored up by the time I ran him down. Sort of forgot to quit beating his ugly face."

"You killed him with your fists?"

"Mm-hmm."

Dan Colt's muscular frame had not gone unnoticed by Lily Dolan. His ice-blue eyes, set in a strong angular face with a squared jaw, told her that if angered he would be a tough customer to deal with.

"Where was your home?" she asked with interest.

"Wyoming. Had a ranch in the Rockies due west of Fort Laramie."

Lily nodded.

Dan continued. "Trailed the killers right through this country. All three were headed southwest in Arizona. Never have figured out why they split up. Took me awhile to track down the third one."

"How long were you married?"

"Little over five years. I was gunslinging . . . bounty hunting, till I met Mary in Wichita. She was the best thing ever happened to Dan Colt. Moved to Wyoming. Bought the ranch. Hung up my guns. Until—"

The hurt filled his eyes again. Lily spoke quickly. "Are you heading for home now?"

"No, ma'am. I don't really want the ranch life now that Mary's gone. Left the ranch in care of some good people."

"What are your plans?" Lily asked, looking toward the shotgunner on the sofa.

"Well, ma'am, there's more to the story. Don't want to bore you."

"No. Please. I want to hear it," she replied, leaning forward on her elbows.

Standing up, Dan said, "Let me check on the horses."

As he strode toward the door, Lily walked to the fireplace and added wood to the fire. As Dan returned, she was feeling the brow of the shotgunner. "He's still got fever, but it doesn't seem to be getting worse."

As Dan Colt and Lily Dolan seated themselves before the fireplace in overstuffed horsehair chairs, he told her of how he was arrested by Holbrook's town marshal. His gunfight with Mary's two killers had been fair, and he was shocked to find the man holding a shotgun on him as he turned to leave. Marshal Logan Tanner was arresting him as one Dave Sundeen, who had resisted arrest and shot the marshal in the process a few months previously.

Lily listened with interest as Dan told her of his trial and how several eyewitnesses pointed him out as the man who had shot the marshal.

"Mrs. Dolan," Dan added, "before the trial the marshal showed me a wanted poster with an artist's sketch of Sundeen. It was *my* face. I knew I didn't have a chance."

"How could it be?" asked Lily, her eyes wide.

"I'm coming to that," Dan replied. "Before I do, let me explain about my childhood. My parents were traveling in Arizona. I don't even know which direction they were going. I was two . . . maybe three years old. A man named Ben Mason and his wife, Katie, were traveling from California to Texas. They happened upon the dead bodies of my parents. Robbers had killed them and plundered what few possessions were in the wagon. They also found *me*. They took me with them to Texas."

"You grew up there?"

"Mm-hmm. Before I was twenty, two men shot down Ben Mason. I vowed to track them down and kill them. I kept my vow, and that's when I learned I had a natural ability with guns. From that point I was a gunslinger until I married Mary."

Lily nodded eagerly. "Go on."

Dan told her of his five year sentence and the trip from Holbrook to Yuma Territorial Prison. He told of how, while in Yuma, he met a convict who had been with the gang the day his parents were robbed and killed.

His eyes widened as he said, "And, Mrs. Dolan, he told me that they took a little blond-headed boy about three years old. One of the outlaws gave him to his wife."

Lily straightened up in the chair. "Your twin!" she exclaimed, popping her hands together.

"Identical."

"And you are looking for him."

"Right."

"How did you get out of prison?"

"Cholera hit everybody but me. Bad water. I was in solitary. No water. A friendly guard, very sick himself, let me out."

"Do you have any idea where Dave—what's he call himself?"

"Sundeen."

"Do you have any idea where he is?"

"I've trailed him to Nogales and back. Report in Durango was that he was three days ahead of me heading north toward Grand Junction. He makes his living as a hired gun. Does some gambling."

Lily cocked her head sideways. "Does he know you are trailing him?"

"Nope. As far as I know, he doesn't even know I exist."

"The law will breathe down your neck till you

bring him in," Lily said. It was a statement, not a question.

"Yep."

"Then I can't detain you. You must get back on his trail tomorrow," said Lily, rising to her feet.

"I can't just ride away, ma'am," Dan said standing up. "You're in trouble, and I'm going to hang around till it's cleared up."

"I really don't—"

"It's a settled matter," Dan said impulsively as he walked toward the door. Donning his hat and pulling on the Mackinaw, he smiled down at Lily Dolan. "I'll ride out to the stagecoach at dawn. If you wouldn't mind fixing me a little breakfast, I'll eat when I get back and be on my way to Welcome." Shaking his head, he said, "That's some name for a town."

As Dan raised the latch Lily said, "I have some extra blankets if you need them."

"I'll be fine, ma'am. Got my bedroll."

"There's a hayloft over the stalls," she said advisedly. "Plenty of hay for the horses and plenty to sleep on."

"We'll be just fine, ma'am. You take care of the shotgunner, and I'll see you a little after sunup."

Lifting the lantern that sat on the table, Lily handed it to the tall man. "The barn is about forty yards in that direction," she said, pointing at a slight angle to the right.

"I'll find it. You lock the door now and get yourself some rest. Good night."

Lily nodded, smiling. "Good night."

The air was biting cold. Lily shivered but stood in the open door, watching the soft glow of the lantern until it disappeared inside the barn.

CHAPTER THREE

Dan Colt was awake at the crack of dawn. His nose was cold. He slipped out of the bedroll and descended the ladder in the dim light. Saddling the black gelding, he tied the bedroll in its place and led the big horse outside.

The wind flopped the brim of his hat as he rode over the bridge and headed south at a brisk trot.

Yellow light was fanning out over the snow-covered peaks to the east as Dan sighted the demolished stagecoach lying on its side in the deep shadows of the canyon. As the big horse cautiously picked its way down the steep slope its rider had chosen, Dan thought about the two robbers who had disappeared yesterday. Would they be back? Whatever it was that they were after lay at the bottom of the canyon. This descent was too treacherous to try in the dark. Maybe they would show up this morning.

Finally reaching the canyon floor, Dan dismounted, ran a quick panorama of his surroundings, then climbed on the wreckage. Peering through the window of the door, he saw the crumpled body of a man. He had seen no one thrown from the coach in the fall. Apparently this was the only passenger. Opening the door and dropping inside, he worked the body loose and hoisted it upward. Balancing it half in and half out, he climbed out and lowered the body to the ground. The pain in his left forearm reminded him of his encounter with the wolf.

Searching for identification, he opened the man's coat. The badge pinned to his shirt was engraved *United States Marshal*. Further search revealed his name to be Wilford Lewis. Dan's first thought was that the coach must have been carrying something of great value. He remembered seeing a few objects fly off the vehicle as it turned over in midair. A quick search of the wreckage convinced him that whatever they were after was lying somewhere near, on the bottom of the canyon.

Stepping around the dead horses, Dan searched the immediate area. There was a mailbag containing a few ordinary letters. A little further investigation produced a satchel with some shirts and underwear, along with a comb and shaving utensils. Nearby, in a clump of bushes, was a shattered box with some tool handles protruding through the splintered openings. Dan was examining the tools when he heard the big black nicker.

The sharp crack of a rifle pierced the early morning air. The bullet whined past Dan's head as the sound of the shot reverberated off the canyon walls. Diving behind the twisted wreckage, he peered through broken boards, searching for the bushwhacker.

Another shot came. The bullet whanged on the metal rim of the wagon wheel above Dan's head and set it spinning. The white puff of smoke came from the same steep slope which Dan had descended earlier. Off to the right of the smoke he caught the glint of a rifle barrel just as it was fired. The bullet splintered wood.

Dan looked at the black gelding, standing twenty feet away on the opposite side of the wreckage. The two bushwhackers were no doubt the survivors of the gang. They wanted something that was being carried in the stagecoach. He must get to the horse and get the rifle from the saddle boot. Bellying down on the cold earth, Dan crept around the wreckage toward the gelding. Two more shots broke the silence, one bullet scattering dirt and the other striking a rock and screaming away. Dan jumped up, slipped the Winchester from the boot, and slammed his back against a giant spruce. The rifles spoke again, shattering bark from both sides of the tree. Levering a shell into the chamber, he swung around the tree and fired up the slope. Both guns returned fire immediately.

Cocking the Winchester again, he waited. Dan reflected on his predicament. He had to get both riflemen before they descended the slope. If they got to the canyon floor, they could circle and come at him from two directions.

Two more shots echoed off the canyon walls, both bullets splitting bark from the tree. Without returning the fire, Dan took a quick look. From the position of the sifting smoke, he could tell that the men had dropped lower on the slope. They were descending now, where the tops of the trees that grew on the canyon floor would hide them.

If the trees would hide them, they would hide *him*. He would catch them as they approached the bottom of the canyon. Swinging around the tree, Dan fired into the dark shadows of the trees along the slope. By the delay of time before the rifles barked again, he knew they were busy picking their way downward. The shots came from lower yet.

Crouching low, Dan Colt rounded the tree to his left and made for the base of the slope. There was a huge boulder right at the place where they would appear. The tall man ran and dropped beside the boulder, on the opposite side from where the bushwhackers would emerge onto the canyon floor.

He waited. The wind sang in the treetops. After several minutes he heard the sound of voices. As the two drew nearer, Dan heard the plan. One would remain behind this large boulder. The other would work his way along the base of the canyon wall and circle around the wreckage. They would catch him in the crossfire. He waited until he heard them crouch down behind the boulder. Dan was exactly on the opposite side.

Knowing that once positioned behind the boulder, they would peer over the top, Dan raised up and pointed the Winchester right where they would lift their heads. Immediately one face appeared. The man's eyes popped and his jaw slacked. He was so stunned he could not find his voice.

"Come out with your hands empty," Dan said in a cold voice. The other one raised up, bringing his rifle to bear. Dan swung the muzzle toward him and squeezed the trigger. The Winchester roared. The man's face spurted blood as the impact flung him hard to his back.

The remaining bushwhacker lifted himself to full height and was swinging his rifle into position. Knowing there was not time to lever in another shell, Dan let the rifle fall and with blurred hand drew and fired his right-hand gun. The man let out a cry and fell dead on his back.

Slowly Dan holstered the Colt, retrieved the rifle, and walked around the boulder. The first man had a blue hole in the middle of his forehead. Blood was trickling into his open eyes. The second man had a bullet in his heart. There was no question. These were the two robbers he had seen veer off the road and disappear into the forest the day before.

What were they after? Dan searched the area of the wreckage one more time. The search revealed nothing new.

By the position of the sun Dan Colt knew it was at least ten o'clock as he rode the black over the bridge on the Tom Dolan ranch. Behind him, on a lead rope, followed the two horses which had belonged to the bushwhackers. One bore the bodies of the outlaws, the other carried the body of U.S. Marshal Wilford Lewis.

As he approached the house, Dan saw a pretty face pull away from the rear window. The door opened and Lily Dolan appeared.

"You had trouble?" she asked, looking beyond Dan to the horses.

"Yes'm. Guess you could call it that," Dan said grimly.

"I was getting worried about you," she said as he dismounted.

"Sorry, ma'am," Dan said with a light smile. "These two *hombres* here detained me for a while. Remember I told you last night that I had killed three robbers?"

"Yes," she said, eyeing the corpses.

"These two here got away yesterday. I figured they would come back after their loot at sunup. Sure enough, they saw me looking through the wreckage and tried to bushwhack me."

"This one was the passenger?" Lily asked, gesturing toward the third body.

"Yes'm," Dan said, wiping a hand over his mustache. "He's a U.S. marshal. Name's Wilford Lewis."

"Was he guarding something on the stagecoach?"

"I don't know. I'm a little puzzled about this. I searched through the wreckage and looked the whole area over thoroughly. Couldn't find a thing of any import. I just can't figure out what they were after."

"The shotgunner is beginning to stir," said Lily with a smile. "You can get some answers when he comes around."

"Good," replied Dan with feeling. "I'm sure he'll get better real fast when he gets a look-see at the pretty nurse he's got."

Lily's face flushed.

"On the other hand, maybe he'll just decide to stay sick a little longer," he said with an impish grin.

"Mr. Colt, if you want some breakfast, you hush up that nonsense and get washed up," she said with a flick of her finger.

"Your husband's not back?"

"No."

"No word from your neighbor?"

"No."

"Any sign of what's-his-name?"

"Mel Curry?"

"Yeah."

"No. But I expect him around soon."

"Why don't I drop you and the children off at the Rice ranch on my way to Welcome? I really don't want to leave you here alone."

"But what about the shotgunner?" Lily asked quickly. "I can't leave him. We will be all right, Mr. Colt."

"I don't like it," Dan said. "Didn't you say that Curry threatened harm to you and the children?"

"Yes, but I—"

"Maybe we could take the shotgunner along," said Dan quickly.

"It would be too much for him, Mr. Colt. We will be all right. Now, you take the horses to the barn, and I'll get your breakfast ready."

Shaking his head, the tall man swung the horses around. Pausing momentarily, he spoke to Lily as she stepped onto the porch. "Guess I better bury these three after breakfast. Any particular spot you want me to use?"

"You're going to have a difficult time, Mr. Colt. The ground is still frozen. But you can pick a spot back behind the barn."

Dan nodded. Leading the horses toward the barn, he called over his shoulder, "I'll be in in about twenty minutes." Lily smiled and closed the door.

Inside the barn Dan laid the three bodies out in an empty stall. He took the saddles and bridles off the outlaws' horses, loosed the cinch of his own saddle, and released the bit from the black gelding's mouth. Climbing into the loft, he forked hay into the manger. As he descended the ladder, he heard Lily's voice. It was pitched high. Though he could not make out her words, Dan caught the angry tone.

Running to the barn door, Dan looked toward the house. Four riders were at the back porch. One of them had dismounted and was standing with one foot on the step. Lily was on the porch, just outside the door. She held the Sharps on the man.

"Mel Curry," Dan said audibly. Though he could not make out the features of the man's face, Curry appeared to be in his middle forties. He was a little less than six feet tall and thickly built. A lighted cigar protruded from his mouth.

Dan eased the barn door open and carefully slipped outside. None of the men was looking in his direction. He ran flat-out to the opposite side of the house and rounded the corner. Cautiously he made his way to the next corner and removed his hat. Poking his nose around the edge, he saw Curry leap for the rifle and wrench it from Lily's grasp. Roughly he slapped her face and pushed her against the wall next to the door. A wash tub fell from its peg and clattered to the porch floor.

Dan took in the situation as he heard Curry say, "Now, look, lady, you tell me where he is, or I'll beat it out of you!"

One of the riders looked in his direction, and he pulled his head back. He heard Lily say in a frantic tone, "I told you. He went to Welcome."

"What's takin' him so long to get back?" Curry's voice bellowed.

As Dan looked again, the big man had both hands palmed against the wall, with Lily in between. His face was no more than ten inches from hers. He had the cigar pointed at her and was blowing smoke in her face. Lily coughed, and Curry slapped her again.

"That's enough!" Dan roared as he stepped into sight. The twin Colts were leveled at Curry. The big man stepped back and eyed Dan viciously. Biting hard on the cigar, he cursed. "Who are you?"

"Abraham Lincoln," said Dan icily. "I've come to free the slaves."

"You butt out, mister!" Curry bellowed.

One of the riders clawed for his gun. The .45 in Dan's left hand roared. The rider toppled to the ground. Another one moved his hand from where it rested on the pommel.

"Go ahead, if you want your supper in Hell tonight!" Dan barked. The rider's face blanched as he slowly placed the hand back on the pommel. Curry started to move. Fixing his ice-water stare on him, Dan snapped, "You stay right where you are, big boy." Curry checked himself.

"You two on the horses," Dan said without looking directly at them, "lift those rifles from their boots and drop them." This done, he said, "Now drop your gunbelts."

As the gunbelts met the ground, Dan said, "Mrs. Dolan, would you pick up their guns and take them in the house, please?"

Lily rubbed her face and gave Mel Curry a fiery look as she stepped off the porch and began gathering the guns.

"Now you drop *yours*, Curry," Dan said, tight-lipped.

Curry rolled the cigar in his mouth. Dan could hear Patty Ruth and Danny whimpering inside the house. Curry's gunbelt fell at his feet as he said, "How do you know my name? I never saw you before."

"I read it once in a book," Dan replied curtly.

"A book?"

"Yeah. A book about snakes. In my book the only thing lower than a green-bellied snake is a yellow-bellied asp who beats up on women."

Curry's face colored floridly. His eyes darkened. Dan could not tell whether the smoke was coming from Curry's eyes or the cigar that parted his lips.

Looking toward the riders, Dan rasped, "You two are going after Dolan's horses and buckboard. Your boss will wait here while you do it."

Curry swore vehemently. "We ain't got no horses and we ain't got no buckb—"

The gun in Dan's right hand roared. Curry's hat flew off. He staggered backward, lifting a hand to his head. His eyes were wide and blinking in astonishment.

"I said I want Dolan's horses and buckboard. And I mean now!" Dan rasped. His face looked like a thundercloud, ready to unleash its fury.

"Okay! Okay!" Curry said nervously. "You boys go get the horses and the buckboard!"

Lily had stored all the guns in the house, including the Sharps, and now was standing on the porch.

"Mrs. Dolan," said Dan, looking in her direction.

"Yes."

"How many horses did you have?"

"Six."

"Were they branded?"

"Yes. They all have Tom's brand."

"You jackals better bring all six," Dan said with authority.

"Do as he says, Ralph," Curry cut in.

"What about Wally?" asked the other rider, looking at the dead man on the ground.

"Take him back to the place. We'll bury him there," Curry answered.

Both riders dismounted and hoisted the dead man, belly down, over the saddle. One of them eyed the butt of the rifle protruding from the boot of the dead man's saddle.

Dan smiled thinly. "If you reach for it, it'll be the last thing you ever do."

Stiffly the two men mounted their horses. Holstering his left-hand gun, Dan strode to the horse bearing the dead man and lifted the rifle from the boot. Fixing his steady eyes on the two riders, he said, "If you honyocks come back with artillery, you'll have to put plugs in your boss's belly so it will hold water. You get my message?"

"We get it," retorted Ralph sourly.

As the horses clomped over the bridge, Dan turned and walked to Mel Curry. "Now, Curry, I'm going to show you what I think of a yellow-bellied reptile who slaps women around."

CHAPTER FOUR

Mel Curry's florid face went white. He shifted the cigar nervously from one side of his mouth to the other. As his breathing became heavier, the smoke grew thicker.

Releasing the leather thongs and unbuckling his gunbelt, Dan handed it to Lily, along with the rifle. He fixed his pale-blue eyes on the thick-bodied man. Although Curry was four inches shorter, Dan would spot him thirty pounds. Ordinarily Curry would have held no fear in facing a fist fight with a man he outweighed. But there was a look of chilled fury in the tall man's eyes that drove a cold blade of fear through Mel Curry's soul.

Behind those livid eyes were thoughts of Carl Fox. A giant of a man himself, Fox had murdered Mary Colt. Dan had dogged his trail until he found him . . . then beat him into eternity with his two fists. Dan Colt had always held bullies in contempt, but a man who would hurt a woman had slithered out of a slime pit.

Curry swallowed hard as Dan stood less than a yard from him. He bit down on the cigar. Curling his lip, he spoke around it. "N-now, look here, mister. I—"

"You like to slap people, Mr. Curry? Why don't you slap *me*?"

Beads of sweat gathered on the heavy man's brow.

"Is Dan gonna beat the tar outta Mel Curry,

Mama?" It was Patty Ruth. She and Danny were standing in the doorway.

Lily said something Dan could not distinguish. "Take the children inside, Mrs. Dolan," Dan said softly, his eyes holding check on Curry.

Both children fussed as their mother ushered them inside. Just as the door closed, Danny was heard to say, "I wanna see Mr. Colt beat the tar outta—" The door slammed shut.

Curry's eyes twitched. "Mr. Colt? You're *Dan Colt*? The gunslinger? Now, listen here. I ain't—"

"My guns are in the house," Dan snapped quickly. "This is a slapping contest. You seem mighty good at slapping a little defenseless woman who doesn't weigh as much as your left leg. Now, why don't you just take a whack at *me*?"

Curry shifted the cigar and muttered something inaudible. Dan did not notice the three faces gathered at the window. The two smaller ones pressed their noses tight against the pane.

From out of nowhere Dan's right hand palmed Curry's heavy face with a loud pop. Curry staggered slightly as Dan backhanded him fiercely. The cigar took flight as Dan caught Curry's face with his left hand, on the rebound. As the heavy man raised his hands to protect himself, the tall man threaded them away and lashed him with a rapid series of open-handed blows and backhands.

Mel Curry fell to the floor of the porch, scattering buckets, tools, and a wash tub. With molten fire flooding through his veins Dan hoisted Curry to his feet, swung him around, and threw him off the porch.

Curry, realizing he was dealing with a bundle of fury, scrambled to his feet and charged Dan Colt. He came with his head lowered like a Mexican bull. The agile Colt sidestepped him and put a hard boot to his posterior. His momentum doubled, Curry crashed into the porch violently.

Gathering himself, he charged Dan again. The tall man met him with a chopping fist to the left ear. Curry rolled in the dirt and raised up on his knees. Before he could get to his feet, the furious Colt charged in, cupped both hands behind Curry's head, and pulling his face downward, brought up his knee savagely.

While the big man rolled around in agony, Dan walked toward the house and picked up the smoking cigar. Curry was on the ground, moaning and holding his hands to his bleeding nose.

Dan straddled him and came down with all two hundred and ten pounds, knees-in-belly. Air gushed from Curry's mouth, spraying Dan with blood. Sitting straddled across the big man's middle, he gripped a fistful of hair with his left hand, holding Curry's head, viselike, to the ground.

"You like to put your cigar in people's faces, don't you?" Dan said with a hot hiss. Curry's eyes were wild with fear.

With his right hand, Dan pointed the red-hot end of the cigar at Curry's mouth. Instantly Curry clamped his mouth shut and pulled his lips tightly together.

"Open your mouth, woman-fighter!" Dan shouted.

Curry tried to shake his head in protest. He could not move it. Dan's grip was like tempered steel. Blood was bubbling from Curry's nose.

"Open your mouth, big, tough woman-handler! I want to show you what it's really like to have a cigar stuck in your face!"

Curry gave a nasal whine. Methodically Dan lowered the burning tip of the cigar and pressed it to the big man's tightly closed lips. The burning flesh made a slight sizzling sound. Curry opened his mouth to cry out. Dan jammed the smoking cigar down his throat and clamped his jaw shut.

Curry bucked and writhed wildly. Tears ran from

his eyes and blood spurted from his nose. He began to gag and choke. Dan held his jaw tight till Curry's face took on a blue tone. Casually he released the grip on his hair and jaw and stood up.

The big man gagged, choked, coughed, and spit cigar fragments as he rolled to his knees. As Dan stood over him, he glanced toward the house. All three faces in the window were smiling broadly. Danny was clapping his hands. Dan smiled back and winked.

As Mel Curry continued choking and spitting, Dan hoisted him to his feet and half-carried him to the water trough at the barn. Letting him drop to his knees, Dan stuck his face in the ice-cold water. "This will make it feel better, Mr. Curry." Dan bobbed his head several times. When he let go, Curry lay prostrate, still gagging.

Dan walked to the house. Patty Ruth leaped off the porch to meet him. Danny was on her heels. "You sure fixed his little red wagon, Dan! Boy, oh, boy! Did you ever—"

"That's enough, Patty," Lily said firmly. "And his name is not Dan, little missy. Do you understand? It is Mr. Colt, to you."

"Yes, ma'am," Patty Ruth said, dipping her chin.

Lily looked up into Dan's sweaty face. "I was afraid you were going to kill him," she said breathlessly.

"Not on an empty stomach." Dan said, laughing.

Stepping into the house, he buckled on his guns and thonged them down. Picking up the rifle that he had taken from the dead rider's saddle boot, he said to Lily, "Mr. Curry is going to help me bury the men in the barn. The marshal probably has kinfolks who would like to be at his burial, but I'm going to have to go ahead with it."

"I'm sure they will understand," Lily replied. "Why don't you let me feed you first?"

After downing a hearty breakfast, Dan picked up

Mel Curry at the water trough. His face was caked with blood. Pushing the thick-bodied man along in front of him, the blond-headed man moved to a tool shed, where he handed a long-handled pickax to Curry. Picking up a shovel for himself, he said, "You can pick and I will dig."

Dan put the two robbers in the same grave. Wilford Lewis was given one by himself. Dan removed the badge and put it in his shirt pocket. He had already placed the identification papers in his saddlebag.

Mel Curry had remained quiet and sullen throughout the entire ordeal. Though the early spring air was nippy at this altitude, Curry had worked up a sweat. He stood mopping his brow while Dan shoveled the loose dirt into the graves.

The sound of horses' hoofs met their ears. Looking toward the corral, Dan saw Curry's same two men run six horses through the gate. Another man followed, driving Tom Dolan's buckboard. He backed the buckboard into the shed, released the team from the doubletree, climbed aboard one of the horses, and rode away.

The other two caught sight of Colt and Curry where they stood in an open area behind the barn.

"You ready to go, boss?" one of them shouted.

"Not till Mrs. Dolan inspects her horses!" Dan answered.

Lily Dolan was summoned. After examining the six animals and informing Dan Colt that she was satisfied, she glared at Mel Curry and said, "I hope this is the end of it, Curry."

Without a word the big man walked to his horse and swung gingerly into the saddle. He sat there a long moment, looking at Lily Dolan with expressionless eyes.

"It *better* be the end of it, mister," Dan rasped.

Curry spoke softly. It was evident that it pained

him to speak. "We'll take our guns now, Colt." His eyes watered as he choked and coughed.

"Whatsa matter with you, boss?" asked Ralph.

Curry flung him a flinty look. "You shut up." Turning back to Colt, who stood by the back porch next to Lily Dolan, he growled, "I said we want our guns."

"Do you know what the penalty is for horse stealing in these parts?" Dan asked in a rough, grating tone. Curry swallowed hard but did not answer.

"Mrs. Dolan could have you and your henchmen hung. You know that?"

Curry cleared his throat carefully. Dan could read a dark hatred in his eyes.

"She's letting you off easy, mister," Dan continued. "All it's costing you this time is your guns. They are Dolan property now."

Curry's eyes flashed with fire. "Now, look here, you—"

Dan walked briskly toward Curry, speaking sharply as he approached. "You want to eat another cigar, mister? I'll be glad to oblige!"

Curry reined his horse sharply, backing the animal several steps. "Okay! Okay! She can keep the guns."

Dan halted. Curry looked toward his two riders. "Let's go, boys."

"Just one minute, Curry!" Dan barked. "You've got one more thing to do."

"What's that?" the big man choked.

"You forgot to tell Mrs. Dolan that you're sorry you slapped her." Dan's jaw was set. Mel Curry was a whipped man. He was not ready to fight Dan Colt again.

Curry spoke softly. "I'm sorry, ma'am."

"Speak up!" Dan said sharply. "She can't hear you!"

"I'm sorry, ma'am."

This time Dan was satisfied with the volume. "You're sorry for *what*?"

Curry cleared his throat. "For slapping you, ma'am."

Lily nodded her head. Her lips were drawn in a tight line. There was a reddish-blue bruise forming on her left cheekbone.

"Now you can go," Dan said firmly.

Curry swung his horse around slowly. "And, Curry . . ."

The big man eyed Dan darkly. "Yeah."

"If you or any of your pack bothers the Dolans anymore, I'm coming after you. I'll hunt you down like a cur dog and kill you."

Without a word the three riders rode away slowly. Dan knew by the malignant look in Curry's eyes the conflict was not over.

As he approached the porch, Lily smiled and said, "Our shotgunner is awake. He wants to talk to you."

CHAPTER FIVE

Dan Colt lowered his muscular six-feet-three-inch, two-hundred-and-ten-pound frame onto a straight-backed wooden chair next to the sofa. The shotgunner looked at him with dull eyes. A smile tugged at the corners of his wide mouth.

"I'm sure glad you're doing better," Dan said, showing his white, even teeth. "We were a mite worried about you."

Lily stood behind Dan looking down at the wounded man. The children flanked their mother on each side.

"I owe my life to you, Mr. Colt," the slender, rawboned man said slowly, ". . . and to the pretty lady, here. Sure do thank you." He adjusted his prone position and winced.

"I take it you and the pretty lady have been talking," Dan said calmly.

"A little," he answered with a slight grunt.

"I guess you know my name," said Dan, "but I don't know yours."

"Charlie." He bit his lip and moved his wounded shoulder. "Charlie Lacy."

Dan judged the Wells Fargo shotgunner to be in his early sixties. Even though his eyes were dull from the strain of the wound, there was a winsome glint about them.

"You've lost a great deal of blood, Charlie," Dan

said with concern. "You need to drink a lot of water. Build up the liquid in your system."

Charlie squinted at Dan. "Looks like you took a bath in a bucket of blood, yourself." A sly smile slid across his lips.

Dan looked down at his blood-spattered shirt. Wiping his hand across his face, he said, "Had a friendly little argument with one of Mrs. Dolan's neighbors."

"Yeah, Mr. Lacy! Dan—I mean . . . Mr. Colt really beat the snot out of him!" Patty Ruth chimed in excitedly. "You shoulda seen—"

"Patty Ruth!" Lily said sharply. "What have I told you about children?"

The dark-haired girl tilted her head downward, looked at her mother morosely, and said in a soft monotone, "Children should be seen and not heard."

"And . . ." Lily gave her a hard look.

"And should speak only when spoken to," Patty Ruth said, looking at the floor.

"You seem to have forgotten your manners," said Lily firmly.

"Yes'm," replied Patty Ruth.

"I saw you whup two *hombres* at one time in Wichita, Colt," Charlie said, looking at Dan.

"You did, huh?"

"Yep. You got *some* temper. Remind me to stay on your good side."

Dan chuckled. "I only lose my temper when I get mad."

Charlie snickered. Lily smiled. "You know me, then?" Dan queried.

"Yep. Seen yuh in three, four gunfights too. *Whew!*" Charlie licked his lips and set his eyes on Lily. "Mrs. Dolan, you ain't never seen nobody fast with a pair a twin Colts till you seen this kid in action!"

"I saw enough today when he handled Mel Curry

with his bare hands," replied Lily. "I wouldn't want to see him use his guns."

"Did you work for Wells Fargo in Kansas?" Dan asked.

"Yep. Rode the route from Kansas City to Wichita for twelve years." Lacy winced again, pulling air inward through clenched teeth. "Holy cats, that hurts!" he said with a twisted face.

"We'd better let him rest, Mr. Colt," Lily interjected. "He's mighty weak yet. I'll fix him some beef broth and hot coffee."

"I could use some of that coffee, myself," said the tall man. He followed Lily to the kitchen area. "I'm sorry, ma'am, about the delay in my getting started for Welcome. I know you must be plenty worried about your husband by now."

"Don't apologize," she said with a warm smile. "All you did was help me out of a tight spot. It certainly wasn't your fault Mel Curry showed up."

Dan eyed the old clock on the kitchen wall. It was twenty minutes to three. "Guess I'd better wait and strike out for Welcome first thing in the morning, ma'am. I do need to talk to Charlie about the robbery and Wilford Lewis and all."

"Certainly, Mr. Colt. Whatever has happened to Tom will probably be no different by morning."

Dan's brow furrowed. He ran his fingers through his thick blond hair. "Uh—ma'am..."

Lily paused at what she was doing at the stove. Tossing a quick glance in his direction, she said, "Mm-hmm."

"I'd really appreciate it if you would call me Dan."

She had turned back to the stove. Over her shoulder she answered, "If you will call me Lily."

"It's a deal, Lily."

The sun was dropping behind the jagged peaks on the western side of the valley when Dan sat down beside Charlie Lacy again. The hot broth had strengthened the wounded shotgunner, and he welcomed Dan's presence.

"Charlie, I need to ask you some questions."

"Figgered on that," Charlie responded with a smile.

"What were the robbers after? I went through everything on the stage. Couldn't find anything worth stopping a stage for."

"They weren't after *what* we were carrying, Dan. It was *who* we were carrying."

"The marshal?"

"Yep. He was headed for Welcome."

"Somebody didn't want him to make it to Welcome?"

Charlie nodded. "Keerect. There's somethin' mighty strange goin' on there, Dan. Fer about three months now I've noticed somethin' peekuliar about Welcome every time I stop there."

"Like what?" Dan asked, leaning forward.

Lily sent the children into the bedroom to play and drew up a chair next to Dan and sat down.

Charlie gritted his teeth, readjusted his position, and said, "People act funny. They used to be warm and friendly."

Dan smiled. "Oughtta be, in a town called Welcome."

"Used to be a gold mine town," Charlie Lacy continued. "There were three rich veins being culled out day and night. Town mushroomed. Saloons were built. Four hotels cropped up. Business was boomin'. Ever'body was gettin' rich."

Charlie winced as he tried to make himself more comfortable, then continued. "Town started out as Ute City. Was just sort of a way station between Durango and Ouray. Nothin' but a tradin' post and a small drinkin' establishment. When gold was discovered and it began to prosper, they changed the name to Welcome."

"Wanted people to come and settle there," Dan said, sinking back in his chair.

"Yep. And shore enough, the people of the town lived up to the name. Was the friendliest bunch o' people you ever met in your life," Charlie said with a wistful look in his dark blue eyes. "Then it happened."

"What's that?" Dan asked.

"Mines began to play out. One by one, all three of 'em emptied out within three, four months. Most folks left. Businesses went broke. Few folks that stayed sorta lived offa each other."

Charlie managed a weak chuckle, shook his head.

"What's so funny?" Dan queried.

"Folks that stayed were still mighty friendly. Used to really enjoy my stops there. Went on that way for nearly two years. Place was always good for a few laughs."

Dan felt of his wounded forearm and thought of the wolf. "What happened, Charlie?"

"Don't rightly know," he said, slowly shaking his head. "One day we rode in as usual, but nobody smiled or joked. Even old Sam Ewing—he handles the mail—was sober as a hangin' judge. He's always had a big smile and a story to tell. People looked at me real funny. There's sort of a tired, fearful look in their eyes.

"It's been this way now fer about three months. When I speak, they say two or three words, if any, and shy away."

Dan's brow wrinkled. "You mean no one will tell you what the problem is?"

"Nope. I remember one day, 'bout a month ago. Bob Tally . . ." Lacy closed his eyes and sniffed and clenched his jaw for a long moment. Gaining control of himself, he continued. "Bob Tally—that was the driver that Mrs. Dolan said you buried—" The older man's lower lip quivered. Looking up at

Dan Colt through tear-blurred eyes, he said, "Bob was my best friend, Dan. He and I—"

As Charlie fought to regain his composure, Lily stood up and walked into the bedroom. Dan leaned over and squeezed the shotgunner's forearm. Tears were now visible on Lacy's weathered cheeks.

"I can't bring your friend back to you, Charlie, but at least I can tell you that the jackals who killed him are clawing their fingers raw on the walls of Hell."

Lily emerged from the bedroom with a large red handkerchief, which she tenderly placed in Charlie's hand.

Once again gaining his composure, Lacy mopped his wet cheeks. "I'm beholden to you for riddin' the world of them killers, Dan. The pretty lady here told me how you kept a wolf from havin' me fer supper too. Seems I owe you a lot, young feller." Charlie was managing a weak smile. "Maybe I kin pay you back someday."

Dan settled back in the chair. "You don't owe me anything," he said, showing his even white teeth in a broad smile. "Feel like talking some more?"

"Shore." Charlie blew his nose softly into the handkerchief. "Bob tried to get Slim Withers away from the others while we were eatin' at the Buffalo Cafe, and Slim avoided him. Kept eyein' some drifters who were settin' around at the tables. Slim's the cook and waiter at the place. He was just plain scared."

"Do you suppose somebody's got the town treed?" Dan suggested soberly.

"Could be," answered Lacy. "Several times I tried to talk with the Fargo agent, Ed Sorenson. He always got a frightful look in his eyes and kept lookin' toward one of the abandoned buildings . . . as if he was expectin' a ghost to jump through its walls."

"Have you gotten any kind of a hint as to what it's all about?" The question came from Lily, whose husband had headed for Welcome four days previously and had not returned.

"Didn't have a thing, ma'am, till Marshal Lewis clumb on the stage at Durango. Before we lit out, he shed a whole lotta light on the mystery."

Dan Colt and Lily Dolan listened intently as the wounded shotgunner related Marshal Wilford Lewis's story. Someone in Welcome had slipped a note to one of Charlie's passengers about ten days ago. The passenger carried the note to the sheriff at Durango. The note had been scribbled hastily and part of it was illegible. The sheriff could make out enough to tell that Welcome's town marshal was in real trouble and needed help. He immediately wired the U.S. marshal's office at Raton. A letter was sent to the marshal at Welcome that Wilford Lewis would be on the Wells Fargo stage out of Durango on Tuesday, April 14.

The only additional information Charlie Lacy had, came from people along the stage route from Durango to Grand Junction.

"Folks say that some people have ridden into Welcome and never been heard from again," Charlie said with an edge of a whisper.

Lily and Dan looked at each other simultaneously.

"Whatever is happening has happened to Tom," she said, her voice quivering.

"Don't jump to conclusions yet," Dan said quickly. "Let me get to Welcome and do some investigating first."

Lily stood up, wringing her hands. "Bill Rice too," she said, biting her lip.

"I know it looks bad, Lily," Dan said as he rose from the chair, "but hang on until I can check it out."

Turning back to Charlie, he said, "Apparently those killers that attacked the stage were sent to make sure the U.S. marshal didn't make it to Welcome."

"That's the way it looks to me," said Charlie.

"The two that came back to the wreckage this morning were bent on making sure Lewis was dead," Dan said half to himself.

The tall man ran his fingers through his thick blond hair as he studied the floor. Looking at Lily, then at the wounded shotgunner, he said, "I've got an idea. Since all the men who were sent to kill Lewis are dead, no one in Welcome knows what happened."

"Yeah?" said Charlie.

"If I pin on Lewis's badge and carry his papers, no one in Welcome will know but what I am Lewis."

"Only one hitch," chided Charlie. "Lewis was supposed to arrive on the stage yesterday."

"That poses no problem. I'll tell them some robbers tried to hold up the stage. The stage went over the cliff. I jumped free. They don't even need to know that all their appointed killers are dead. I'll tell them some of the robbers got shot . . . others scattered. The important thing is, if they think I'm the U.S. marshal, they will be mighty careful. They'll know if anything happens to me, the next thing will be a visit from the army."

"Good thinkin' fer a wet-nose kid," said Charlie with a furtive grin.

"I'll even ride one of the killers' horses into Welcome," Dan said with a sly look. "That'll make it look even better."

As the sun fell behind the jagged peaks and the clouds burst into flame, Dan Colt swung the ax the final time, splitting the log with one blow. After depositing the ax in the tool shed, he began loading the split logs into the crook of his right arm with his left hand.

Danny Dolan, who had been standing a safe distance from the chopping area, now moved in and said, "C'n I carry some wood, Mr. Colt?"

"Sure, Danny," said the tall man. "C'mere."

Curling both arms, the little fellow smiled at Dan Colt as he placed two logs against his chest. "Someday I'm gonna be big and strong like you, Mr. Colt," he said, his eyes dancing.

"Sure, Danny. You'll probably be bigger and stronger."

"An' you know what I'm gonna do when I get big?"

"What are you going to do?"

"I'm gonna beat the snot outta Mel Curry, just like you did!"

Dan smiled. Standing to full height, his own arm loaded with wood, he said, "Let's take this to the house, partner."

Patty Ruth was waiting at the door to let them in. As Dan stacked the wood by the fireplace, Lily spoke from the kitchen area. "All right, everybody. Get to the table."

While Dan Colt and the children wolfed down the meal, Lily fed Charlie, who was still confined to the sofa.

Dan was sipping a cup of coffee when Lily took her own place at the table and dabbed a small portion of cold food on her plate.

Dan could see worry lining her lovely face. He knew her insides must be churning like a grist mill. She was on the verge of tears, and he was nonplused.

Suddenly Danny solved it for the tall man. In his boyish manner he said, "Mama, don't worry. Mr. Colt will bring Papa home. Mr. Colt can do *anything!*"

Lily touched the boy with a loving look and smiled broadly. "I'm beginning to think you're right, son. Mr. Colt is quite the man. If anybody can find your father and bring him home, it's Mr. Colt."

Dan put his hand on top of the boy's head. Tousling his hair, he said, "I bet I'm not half the man your father is, Danny."

After supper Dan and the boy went to the barn to see to the horses. The night was cold. As Dan closed the barn door, Danny looked up in the light of the lantern and said, "Could I ride on your shoulders back to the house, Mr. Colt?"

Dan studied his face by the flickering flame. He had once dreamed of having a son. For a fleeting moment he thought of Mary. Scenes of bygone days on their Wyoming ranch raced across his memory. His thoughts returned to the present as Danny spoke again. "I'm not too heavy. Could I, Mr. Colt?"

Dan lifted his hat and placed it on the boy's head. It fell over the stocking cap he wore and surrounded his ears. Hoisting Danny to a sitting position on his shoulders, he picked up the lantern and started toward the house. "Bet you can see for *miles* up here, can't you, Mr. Colt?" the boy said, laughing.

"Probably at least a hundred, Danny," he answered lightly.

As they neared the house, Danny spoke again, "Yes, sir, Mr. Colt. When I grow up, I want to be *just like you!*"

After the children were in bed, the three adults sat up and talked for a while. Soon Charlie's head began to bob, and his eyes drooped.

Dan stood up and stretched. "I'll just spread out here on the floor, ma'am. If Charlie doesn't snore too loud, I'll get me a good night's sleep."

Being provided with a pillow and blankets, Dan lay for a long while, just watching the dying embers in the fireplace. He could hear Lily in the bedroom. Periodically she would sniff and blow her nose in a subdued manner. In the deep of the night, he made Lily a silent promise. *If Tom is alive, I will bring him home to you. If someone has taken his life, Lily, they will pay. You can bank on it.*

CHAPTER SIX

Three days before Dan Colt foiled the attack on the Wells Fargo stage, Dave Sundeen rode into Welcome, Colorado. The town was situated nine thousand feet above sea level, between two mountains, which both lifted their heads above timberline. No one had seen the bare red earth on the treeless peaks since the first snowfall in early September.

The morning sun was level with the eastern peak as Sundeen cast his gaze the length of the town. Six blocks. The business section covered both sides of the street. To the right and left houses were built on the mountain sides, accessible by deep-rutted wagon trails.

A strange feeling crept over the tall gunslinger as the big buckskin gelding carried him adjacent to the first buildings. He eyed the vacant structures, some with doors and windows boarded. Other unused buildings revealed doors sagging on twisted hinges, while broken shards of glass clung recklessly to dilapidated window frames.

Even the business establishments which showed evidence of activity displayed a lack of care, as paint peeled from the weather-worn false fronts, and faded signs swung on rusty hooks.

Sundeen made a mental note that the only sign with fresh paint was the one he had seen just before entering the town. The one that read:

WELCOME
Pop. 97

The paint was thin, and it was easy to see that the population had once been something in four figures.

While Dave Sundeen's sixth sense prodded him uneasily, wary eyes followed him through the inch-wide cracks of a boarded window. A back door opened and closed quietly as booted feet ran unnoticed behind the buildings.

The Rockaway Saloon seemed to be the only one in business. Sundeen found it near the end of the second block, directly across the street from the Wells Fargo office. The stagecoach was about to pull out. As he swung his leg over the buckskin's back, he heard the shotgunner say, "Ed, I ain't never seen you like this! You and this whole town been actin' strange fer weeks!"

As he wrapped the reins around the hitching rail, Dave Sundeen cast a glance across the street. The big bald man called Ed was wiping his face with a bandanna as his eyes darted left and right nervously. The rawboned shotgunner shook his head vigorously as he climbed up and dropped onto the seat beside the driver.

"Let's go, Bob," he said with a note of disgust.

"See you next time, Charlie," Ed said, trying to smile.

In a darkened second-story window just above the Wells Fargo office three men peered through a dirt-stained window. The one gasping for breath said, "Looks like a good prospect, Huey. He rode in alone."

Huey Stokes was a dark-skinned man in his early thirties. He was thin, with sharp features and a natural scowl, which, coupled with narrow-set black eyes, struck fear into many a man. He was a gunslinger of the first order. He wore a thin mustache, which looked like drainage from his nostrils.

The third man, Hector Penney, was big and thick-bodied. He had a fair complexion and straw-yellow hair. Hector studied the tall man as he alighted from the buckskin.

"Looks like a gunslinger, Huey. He's built strong, though."

"Let's go get him, Huey," said the runner excitedly.

"Not yet, Louie," said Huey quickly. "We'll let the stage get out of town first. Looks like he's going into the saloon. Louie, you run over there and give Hank the signal."

Louie bounded out the door without a word.

The two men watched as Louie stepped out in the street and crossed to the Rockaway. The sound of the stagecoach died away as the tall man pushed open the door of the saloon. Louie Stokes, who was twelve years younger than his brother, was slender and lithe. He followed the tall blond gunslinger through the door.

Sundeen approached the bar, flipped his flat-crowned hat off the back of his head. It hung between his shoulder blades by the knotted cord under his chin.

"Whisky," said Sundeen, fixing his pale-blue eyes on Hank Beaman, who faced him from behind the bar. Without a word the bartender poured a shot glass half full and set the bottle within the tall man's reach. As Sundeen tossed off the glass, Louie Stokes stood at the end of the bar next to the door. He caught Beaman's eye, shifted his gaze to Sundeen and back to the bartender. Beaman nodded slowly. Louie walked to one of the tables and sat down.

Several men were seated at tables, playing cards. Dave stood alone at the bar, studying the room in the mirror behind the bar. Hank Beaman pulled out a white handkerchief and mopped his brow. Sundeen hardly noticed Beaman's gesture, but almost immediately chairs began to scrape on the uneven wooden floor and men began to file out the door. Sundeen replenished his empty glass, keeping his back to the table area.

When the door swung shut, Sundeen could see two men seated at one table. One of the two men was the one who had come through the door behind him. He downed the second shot, dropped a coin on the bar, and turned to leave. Just then the door opened and Huey Stokes entered, followed by Hector Penney.

Something in Stokes's eyes touched a nerve in Dave Sundeen, but before it had registered fully, Hank Beamen's big voice bellowed, "Hold it right there, mister!"

The tall man turned around slowly, to face a double-barreled shotgun, glaring at him like two threatening eyes. Both hammers were cocked.

"I think you boys oughtta take that sign down out there on the edge of town. There's really not too much around here to make a fella feel welcome." Dave Sundeen's face was fixed in hard lines.

"See if you can touch the ceiling," Beaman said evenly.

Dave raised his hands. Huey Stokes lifted the twin Colt .45s from their holsters and laid them on the bar. "Have a seat," he said, pointing to the table where Louie and a lean man with a tied-down iron sat. It was only a few feet from the bar.

Reluctantly the tall man seated himself as Huey pulled out a chair and straddled it backward.

"Now, what do you want?" Sundeen asked icily.

"We have a little job for you," Huey answered with a twisted smile. "Ever work in a gold mine?"

"I'm not looking for a job," Dave answered with irritation.

Hector Penney guffawed. "The job's lookin' fer you, though!" Penney looked at Huey Stokes. "He looks husky enough to outwork any two of the others."

"The boss will be glad to see this one," spoke up Louie.

The slender man with the big gun on his hip looked at Dave Sundeen with narrowed eyes, as if studying his features. As yet he had said nothing.

Sundeen reflected on his predicament. He had been in tight spots before. The best thing was to keep his head, prepare as much as possible for a fast move at the proper time, and get them relaxed by appearing to go along with their scheme. His back was to Hank Beaman, who remained behind the bar. The shotgun rested on the bar, held loosely in his meaty hands.

The unobtrusive gunslinger sat to his left. Louie Stokes was directly opposite. Huey sat backward on the chair to his right. Penney was standing a few inches behind Huey, who nonchalantly rocked his chair back and forth.

"Mind if I take this coat off?" said Sundeen, easing out of the chair. Penney dropped his hand to his gun. "Go easy, big boy," Dave said as he slipped out of the short-waisted sheepskin coat. Carefully he draped it over the back of his chair. Before he dropped back onto the chair, he eyed the shotgun. Beaman was barely touching it. The barrel protruded over the edge of the bar about twelve inches. Dave gauged the distance between himself and the bartender and eased back into the chair.

"What gold mine you boys talking about?" Dave asked calmly.

While the cold eyes of the man to his left scrutinized his features, Dave listened as Huey Stokes told of one of the deserted mines having been closed as a ruse. When the other two petered out, one right behind the other, Clyde Tuter, who owned the third mine, knew it was dangerous to be the only mine operator still in business. Feelings were running high and the atmosphere was tense. Tuter feared that the other mine operators would kill him and move in. Taking the foreman, Kyle Waite, into his confidence, Tuter cautiously manipulated the operation and made it look like his mine had also played out. He bought off his workers with saddlebags full of nuggets. They went along with the ruse and rode out of town the day Tuter closed the mine.

Tuter's plan was to let the town die out and wait till the other mine operators left the country. After a safe period of time had elapsed, he would return and open up the mine. Kyle Waite was to return as foreman when the mine reopened. They bided their time at Ouray.

Nearly two years passed, and Waite was urging Tuter to reopen the mine. Tuter stood firm to hold off another year. Kyle Waite arranged an "accident," and Clyde Tuter was killed. Waite hired a couple dozen gunslingers, who rode into the town and besieged its ninety-seven remaining citizens.

A twenty-four-hour guard was established, to ensure that no one left the town. At all times the gang held at least three hostages in the old abandoned Fireside Hotel. Each day new hostages were rotated. When the stagecoach came through, its crew and passengers were allowed to come and go as usual. The townspeople knew that if they tried to reveal the situation, one or more of the hostages would be killed.

Mail went out as usual, to keep suspicion from being aroused. Of course it was censored first.

Roy Sherman, the town marshal, was held a prisoner in his own jail until three days ago. Kyle Waite decided he was a potential hazard to the operation. Sherman disappeared. One of the gunslingers now wore the badge. If anyone passing through asked questions, Sherman had resigned and gone back East.

Captives were garnered to do the heavy work in the mine from drifters and others who passed through

Welcome alone or in small groups. The mine was nestled in a mountainside about a mile southeast of town. Its remote location brought the chances that the operation might be discovered to a minimum.

By keeping the operation of the mine a secret and using virtual slave labor, Kyle Waite was becoming fabulously rich. His henchmen were more than well paid. The whole gang was happy.

"So I am going to become one of your slaves, is that it?" Dave Sundeen asked disgustedly.

"That's the size of it," said Huey Stokes without feeling.

"Isn't your boss smart enough to realize that one of these days somebody is going to come around investigating the disappearance of some of these travelers?"

"Yep," said Huey with a chuckle. "Some of the investigators are now working in the mine!" A hoarse billow of laughter developed around the table.

"But sooner or later," said Dave firmly, "the law is going to come around."

"Kyle's ready for that too," interjected Hector Penney.

"Yeah," added Louie Stokes. "A letter came from the U.S. marshal's office in Raton, addressed to our deceased lawman here. There's a U.S. marshal man comin' here to do some investigatin'. He's comin' up on the Fargo stage. Kyle has hired some real tough boys to ride down close to Durango and—"

"I don't think we need to be telling this bird everything we know, Louie!" snapped Huey.

A sour look twisted Louie's face. "Aw, shucks, Huey. What difference does it make? He'll be in irons ennyhow."

"You just pack it in and let *me* do the talking, little brother."

Louie scowled at Huey wordlessly.

Taking advantage of the silence, the rawboned

gunslinger who sat at Sundeen's left spoke and said, "I've got an idea, Huey."

Huey rocked his chair back. "What's that?"

"I think I know this *hombre*," he said, looking at Sundeen. Bracing Dave with cold gray eyes, he said, "Your name Colt?"

Returning the cold look, Sundeen said, "Nope."

"I'm sure I know you. I'd swear—"

"What's *your* handle?" Dave asked, lips drawn tight.

"Royce. Lester Royce. Mean anything to you?"

"Nope."

"It's been seven or eight years," said Royce, "but I seen you in El Paso. Watched you outdraw and kill three men at one time. We rode north to the New Mexico border together."

"I never saw El Paso till four years ago," Dave said grimly.

"What was your idea?" Huey questioned Royce.

"Just thought as fast as he is with a gun, we might see if Kyle would want to put him on the payroll."

"He says he ain't— Who'd you say? Colt?"

"Yeah, Dan Colt," replied Royce.

"Well, that being the case, we'll just put that broad back to digging gold." A wicked grin curled Huey's mouth.

In the course of the conversation Dave had turned his head far enough to the right to check on the bartender's position. He was leaning, elbows on the bar. The shotgun had not been moved. Beaman was not touching it. His twin .45s were still lying on the bar.

Louie, who sat directly opposite at the table, was unarmed. Penney still stood directly behind Huey, who sat astraddle his chair, incessantly rocking back and forth. Dave Sundeen knew he would probably never be in this good a position for escape again. A whisky bottle rested near his right hand. Lester Royce had his hands palm down on the table, his gun hand next to Dave.

As the wicked grin curled Huey's mouth, Dave waited for his chair to rock backward. In one smooth, lightning-fast move he picked up the whisky bottle, lashed it down savagely on Lester Royce's gun hand, and booted Huey's off-balance chair. He was gambling that it would take the heavy-set bartender two or three seconds to shift his bulk off his elbows and grasp the shotgun.

Royce howled with pain as the heavy bottle shattered on his hand. Huey slammed into big Hector, knocking his feet from under him. Dave leaped to his feet and, jumping sideways, flung his coat from the back of the chair into Beaman's face. The shotgun jerked and roared, ripping into Lester Royce, who was in the line of fire. Dave palmed both .45s from the bar, spun around, and shot Huey Stokes between the eyes as he brought his gun to bear. A second shot slammed through Hector Penney's heart. The gun slipped from Penney's fingers as he toppled dead on top of Huey Stokes.

Hank Beaman was fumbling underneath the bar, reaching for a pistol. As he lifted it upward, Sundeen shot him twice. The heavy man went back stiff-legged against the shelves behind the bar. Bottles and glasses fell, shattering with the impact.

Dave spun around in time to see Louie Stokes pull the gun from Royce's holster and raise the muzzle.

"Don't do it, kid," Dave said, both guns lined on Louie.

The boy hesitated, then thumbed back the hammer. Dave's voice pierced the air. "Don't make me do it, kid!" The choice was clear in Louie's eyes. It was do or die. Dave Sundeen had no scruples about killing a grown man who threw a gun on him. Taking out a kid who had yet to see his twentieth birthday was something else.

The muzzle of the gun in Louie's hand was not yet lined on the tall man. "Put the gun down." Sundeen's voice was flat and firm.

"You killed my brother!" screamed Louie.

"Only because I had to." Dave regarded the door from the corner of his eye.

"Ain't nobody comin' through that door," Louie said with half-parted lips. His face was set in hard lines. "Huey gave orders to stay out."

"Kid," said Dave pleadingly, "drop the gun. I don't want to kill you."

"You mean so you can just ride away, don't you? You killed Huey and you're gonna pay!" As he said it, Louie squared the muzzle on Sundeen. Dave fired, aiming at the shoulder. However, as Louie shifted the gun, he dropped downward, and the bullet seared along the left side of his skull, biting deep. He collapsed to the floor in a heap. While blue smoke hung in the air, Sundeen made his way to the door. Holstering his left-hand gun, he cracked the door and peered through the opening. No one was on the street. His big buckskin stood alone at the hitching rail.

Widening the opening, he looked again. He remembered the strange feeling when he had ridden into town. There were men in those abandoned buildings. If he tried to ride out, they would cut him down. His eyes shot across the street to the steep incline and the houses that dotted the mountainside. His only hope was to ride up that mountain.

Pushing the door shut, Sundeen returned to the bar, where his sheepskin coat clung to the spout of a beer keg. Slipping into the coat, he flipped his flat-crowned hat to his head and quickly reloaded both guns. He took one long look at the lifeless heap of jumbled bodies, crouched low, and darted out the door. As he mounted and wheeled the buckskin, men appeared from the abandoned buildings like cockroaches emerging from hollow walls.

As the big buckskin bounded across the street, bullets bit into frozen earth, whined wildly, and Dave Sundeen was gone.

CHAPTER SEVEN

The heavy darkness was giving way to morning's early gray as Dan Colt rose stiffly from the floor and folded his blankets. Heaping blankets and pillow on a chair, he piled some wood chips in the fireplace and struck a match. The chips smoked, burst into flame, and cracked against the cold air in the room. When the fire was well founded, he added logs.

By the time Lily Dolan appeared on the scene, rubbing sleep from her eyes, the tall blond man had built a fire in the stove, heated water, and shaved. He was running a comb through his hair when she said sleepily, "Morning, Dan. Did you sleep all right?"

"Like an innocent babe," he answered with a smile.

"You may have slept like a babe," a raspy voice chided from the sofa, "but you snored like an old grizzly!"

Dan turned to meet Charlie Lacy's winsome smile. "What do you mean, you old coot?" he retorted with a wry grin. "You were sleeping so sound, all the Mexicans at the Alamo could have charged through here and you wouldn't have known it!"

After socking away a healthy breakfast, Dan Colt stepped out into the crisp morning air. He lifted his coat collar against the cold wind and entered the barn. After forking sufficient hay and breaking the ice in the water trough, he saddled a roan belonging to one of the dead outlaws. He chose the roan because it would be quickly and easily identified. It was imperative that whoever had sent the killers after Wilford Lewis believe that Dan was Lewis.

As he led the roan toward the house, Dan pondered on what awaited him at Welcome. He just might be riding into a rattlesnake nest.

The children were seated at the breakfast table as he entered the house. He pinched Patty Ruth's left ear and tousled Danny's hair. Both children giggled and returned to their food.

Lily was seated beside the sofa shoveling scrambled eggs into the shotgunner's mouth. "He'll allow you to do this forever if you'll let him," Dan said to Lily as he drew up a chair.

Charlie shifted the eggs to one side of his mouth, smacked his lips, and spoke around the eggs. "Yer jist jealous, sonny. You'd give yer big toenail to git her to coddle you a leetle bit." He swallowed, licked his lips. "Only she has a natural magnetism toward a real *he*-man. Long as I'm around, you ain't got a chance. And besides that—" Lily fingered a biscuit into Charlie's mouth and palmed it firmly. He coughed and choked, removing biscuit fragments. "Whut you tryin' to do, woman? Choke a feller to death?"

Dan laughed. Lily falsified a stern look and said, "Okay, mister *he*-man. From now on you can feed yourself!" She placed a steaming cup of coffee in his hand and walked toward the kitchen.

"Aw, now, Lily," Charlie sputtered, "you know you find me irresistible!" As his broad smile faded, the older man looked at Dan Colt. "Guess yer about to leave, huh?"

"Yep. Charlie, how long do you think it'll be till you can ride into Durango?"

"Two, three days, son. Why?"

"I've got a feeling whatever is going on at Welcome might take more'n one man to handle. If I'm not back by the time you feel up to it, will you take one of those horses out in the barn and ride to Durango?

Wire the U.S. marshal's office in Raton and tell them to send some reinforcements. Okay?"

Charlie Lacy nodded his angular head. "Sure will, Dan. Wish I could ride up there with you now."

"I think I can bluff my way for a while," said Dan, "but I might not be able to make a career of it."

"If I don't get to the Fargo office purty soon, they gonna be sendin' a search party after the stagecoach," said Charlie thoughtfully. "I'll be on my way as soon as I kin."

Dan stood up and checked the papers in his shirt pocket. The shotgunner observed the shield pinned to the tall man's vest. "Thet badge looks mighty good on you, son. Mebbe you shoulda been a lawman."

Gripping Lacy's hand, Dan said, "Luck, pardner."

The heavy lines in the corners of Lacy's eyes squeezed together. "Thanks, again, Dan. I owe my life to you."

The tall man smiled. His spurs jingled as he walked to the table. "You two take care of your mother, won't you?"

Patty Ruth shoved back her chair and flung her arms around Dan's slender waist. After clinging for a moment, she tipped her head back and studied his face. "You will bring my father home, won't you, Mr. Colt?"

"I sure will, honey," the tall man replied, as if there was no doubt.

Danny stood up in his chair and extended his arms. As he hugged Dan Colt's muscular neck, he said, "When I grow up, I want to be just like you!"

A hot lump leaped to Lily's throat. Blinking against the moisture gathering in her eyes, she moved quickly and coiled her arms around Dan's chest. As she tilted her face upward, the tears found her cheeks. "Dan, I . . ." She swallowed hard. "There is no way to thank you. I just hope somehow you know—"

Dan laid a rawboned finger on her lips. "I *do* know, Lily. If Tom is alive, I'll bring him home."

Dark clouds covered the sky as the red roan carried its rider over the bridge. Dan turned in the saddle. He waved to the mother and children, who stood huddled together on the porch. As the tall evergreens took them from his view, he squared himself in the saddle and spurred the gelding's sides.

Kyle Waite stood over Louie Stokes's unconscious form, observing the deft movements of Dr. Farley's hands. He had lost count of the days since the stranger had shot down four of his most able men and had left Louie with a .45 caliber crease in his skull. The kid had been unconscious ever since.

Waite was a big, swarthy, formidable man. His ruthlessness was exceeded only by his greed. He had murdered Clyde Tuter in order to gain control of the mine. Kidnaping and forcing men to slave in his mine never disturbed his sleep. He would be rich and powerful at all costs.

As he looked down at Louie Stokes with cold, expressionless features, he held no compassion for the kid. He had one concern. The stranger had killed four men and escaped. Waite had to repeatedly correct himself. The stranger had not killed Les Royce. Somehow Hank Beaman had shot Royce in the fracas. Still, he blamed the stranger for Royce's death.

Waite's riders had chased the man up the mountain, but the big buckskin he forked was too much horse. He got away clean.

No doubt Huey had attempted to capture the man for labor in the mine. How much had Huey told him? Everything Waite had fought and killed for was at stake if word got out about his operation.

Who was this stranger? There was no doubt he was a gunslick. A mighty good one. No average trail hand could have outmaneuvered, outsmarted, and outshot those four hard cases.

A quick investigation revealed that the only men in Welcome who got a look at the man's face were those who encountered his guns in the saloon.

The answer to his identity, or at least his description, lay with Louie Stokes. The man had to be tracked down and killed before he spread the word about the mine. Waite had sent two men into Ouray to fetch Dr. Hal Farley. The physician was not aware of the situation at Welcome. He had been ushered into the room at the Mayflower Hotel where Louie had been bedded down and had been by his side for nearly three days.

Kyle Waite also had another problem on his mind. He had hired five men to intercept the Wells Fargo stage and kill the U.S. marshal enroute to Welcome. They were to do it near Durango and make it look like robbery. This would steer any investigation away from Welcome. The stage had not arrived, but neither had the men. Waite's nerves were riding the edge of panic.

Dr. Farley dropped the bloody bandages into a cardboard box near the bed. Standing up, he stretched his thin frame and turned to Waite. "There's nothing more I can do. Mr. Waite. I really must get back to town."

Waite started to object. He could detain Farley, but that would soon bring someone nosing around. He must let Farley go.

"What do you think, Doc?" Waite asked huskily.

"There is no question he has a serious concussion. I have no way of knowing the extent of the damage internally. He may wake up at any time. He may not wake up at all. It would be risky, but I could take him with me in the surrey. But I must get back to Ouray."

Kyle Waite's head snapped back. "Er . . . ah

". . . no, Doc. You'd better not try that. What can we do for him?"

"Keep him warm. The bandages must be changed every day. I'll leave plenty. As soon as possible after he awakes . . . if he does . . . I want to see him. Is there a woman about who can care for him?"

"Yes, sir, Doc. Yes, sir. We'll see to it," Waite said hastily.

Hal Farley shouldered into his coat, donned his fedora, and picked up his bag.

Kyle Waite stood in the doorway of the hotel and watched the surrey head north out of town.

Dan Colt had not been in the saddle half an hour before it started to snow. Dark clouds were hanging low, obscuring the peaks above timberline. The piercing wind stung his face with tiny ice crystals. It was coming straight out of the north. The roan showed reluctance to proceed into the driving storm and began to fight the bit.

The tall man struggled with the horse and the storm for what seemed a full hour. Frequently he had to brush the snow and ice from his face. He knew the Rice ranch had to be just ahead. In fact it seemed that he should have come upon it before now. Lily said it was off the road to the left. It was a white house with a large unpainted barn.

Dan pulled his eyes to narrow slits against the stubborn wind. Carefully he guided the roan along the road and studied the blurred landscape. The horse continued struggling against the bit and insisted on trying to turn his rump toward the wind.

Within moments the Rice ranch came into view. Dan veered the roan off the road and presently passed through the gate. Wiping snow from his eyes, he studied the house. There was no smoke coming from either chimney. Stepping from the saddle, he bent his head against the wind and made his way to the door. Dan noted that there were no footsteps in the snow, indicating that no one had left the house recently.

When he received no answer to his knock, he turned the knob and the door came open. There was no sign of life inside the house. Everything was in order, including the solitary bed, which was made up neatly.

Dan examined the fireplace and found a small deposit of live coals. Quickly he made his way to the stove. A few dying embers remained in the pit, giving off a soft red glow. Mrs. Rice had not been gone more than a couple of hours. The wind howled around the house like the cry of a wounded beast.

The tall man opened the door aversely and stepped out into the storm. He led the snow-laden roan to the barn. Once out of the driving wind, the gelding shook itself vigorously, scattering snow over frozen manure and straw. Dan examined the stalls. Four horses stood lazily in their respective places. There were three empty stalls. Two had been unoccupied for some time. One of them revealed fresh droppings, no more than two or three hours old.

Dan Colt deliberated on the situation. The storm had hit less than two hours ago. Wherever Mrs. Rice had gone, she had left before the weather had unleashed its fury. Where had she gone? To a neighboring ranch? Possibly. If so, which direction? If she had taken the road south, they would have met. Suddenly it came over him like ice water. *Welcome!* She had gone to find her husband.

Hurriedly Dan pulled a dusty burlap sack off a nail and wiped the saddle dry. "I hate to do this to you, old boy, but we gotta buck that storm some more," he told the horse morosely. "That lady may be holed up somewhere out there."

The storm showed no signs of subsiding as Dan swung the big barn door shut and climbed astride the roan. Horse and man cocked their heads sideways and headed into the norther.

An hour passed.

And another.

Dan scrutinized the road ahead of him. All at once his eyes picked up hoofprints in the snow. Peering through the blur of driving whiteness, he saw a dark-colored horse hunched beneath a tree, rump to the wind. It was off the road to the right, about twenty yards. The empty saddle was covered with snow.

Reining in next to the riderless mount, he began scanning the area for signs of the rider. Vague footprints formed a straight line deeper into the forest.

Dismounting and flicking ice from his mustache, the tall man followed the footprints into the thickness of the trees. He had walked about fifty yards when he saw a cave, nestled at the base of a giant rock formation. The rider definitely had taken shelter in the cave.

Pausing at the opening, he shouted, "Hello in the cave!" He waited a few seconds. No answer. "Hello! There in the cave. Are you all right?"

The noise of the wind made it difficult to hear. Dan bent down and stepped inside. It was pitch black. "Hello!"

Dan thought his ears detected the familiar double click of a revolver being cocked. "Mrs. Rice?" he said quickly.

"Who is it?" The voice was feminine and frightened.

"My name is Dan Colt, ma'am. I'm a friend of Lily Dolan's. I'm on my way to Welcome. Trying to find Tom. Lily asked me to stop by your place and check on you. I know your husband went looking for Tom and hasn't returned. When I saw that you had left this morning, I figured you probably were on your way to town."

Nellie Rice crawled toward Dan out of the

darkness. Her teeth were chattering, and the gun was shaking in her hands. A woolen scarf was draped over her head. The hair exposed just above her forehead was soaked. Her coat was wet. "I was about blind in the storm," she said. "Figured I must have missed the road. Should have been to town by now."

"It just seems like longer in a storm," Dan said advisedly. "Your horse kept you on the road. How did you find this cave?"

"I could see the tall rocks above the trees. Just figured there had to be some kind of shelter."

Dan looked at her with concern. Nellie Rice was probably in her mid-forties, he surmised. She was pretty, in spite of the faint lines that were forming on her forehead, around her eyes, and at the corners of her mouth. "Ma'am, you are really wet. Is your coat soaked all the way through?"

Nellie bit down in an effort to stop her teeth from chattering. "I'm afraid so, Mr.—"

"Colt, ma'am. Dan Colt."

"I'm glad you found me, Mr. Colt," she said, trying to smile.

"Ma'am, we've got to get you dried out as soon as possible." Peeling off his Mackinaw, he shook the snow from it. "Take your coat off and get into this."

"I can't take your coat—" Nellie's eyes fell on the shield pinned to his vest. "You're a U.S. marshal!"

"Yes, ma'am. I . . . I mean no, ma'am," Dan stammered. "That is to say, uh . . ." He wiped his hand over his angular face. "I'll explain that to you later. Right now I want to get this coat on you."

Slipping off her coat, Nellie wrapped the heavy Mackinaw around her slender frame. "Almost goes around me twice," she said with chattering teeth. Her eyes dropped to the left sleeve hanging limply at her side. "What happened to this sleeve, Mr. Colt?" she asked, lifting it upward.

"Timber wolf and I met on the same path," Dan

said calmly. "We had a little dispute as to who had the right of way."

"Since you're still here, I assume you won," she said, lips curling upward.

"Yep."

Dan turned and looked at the falling snow. The wind had diminished somewhat. Facing Nellie Rice once again, he said, "Your place is about eight miles from Welcome. Right?"

"Closer to nine."

"Then we can't be more than a mile or two from town," Dan said, looking back at the snow.

"I really can't say," said Nellie, pulling the collar tightly around her neck. "With the snow blanketing everything and the wind forcing it into my face, I lost all sense of where I was."

"I've either got to build a fire here, or get you to town in a hurry," Dan said, shaking the moisture from his hat. "Sure can tell it's a spring snow. Really full of water."

"By the time you could get a fire going and get me dried out, we could probably be to town," Nellie said shakily.

Agreeing that she was right, Dan helped her back to her horse. The chill bit at his lean frame as they made their way northward. He was glad the wind had subsided. The snow was falling almost straight down now.

As they rode side by side, Dan filled Nellie in on all that had happened since the wreck of the stagecoach. She understood and would go along with his masquerade as U.S. Marshal Wilford Lewis.

The snow had all but stopped falling when Nellie raised a blue finger and pointed straight ahead. "Welcome," she said in a matter-of-fact tone.

Dan knew he would not be.

CHAPTER EIGHT

The clouds hung low but had lightened in color as Dan Colt and Nellie Rice rode past the sign which read:

WELCOME
Pop. 97

It was partially covered with snow, but Dan could make out the lettering. *Crazy name for a town,* he said to himself.

The tall man's eyes shifted warily back and forth as the duo moved slowly up the street. Charlie Lacy had described it well. Most of the buildings were boarded up or in shambles, resembling a ghost town. No doubt they were haunted . . . with the memories of better days. Unseen scrutinizing eyes followed the pair as they approached the Mayflower Hotel.

"There's smoke coming out of this one," Dan said as he reined the roan toward the hitching rail. "We'll check in here."

Two rough-looking men sat on horsehair chairs in the hotel lobby as the tall, broad-shouldered man assisted the small woman through the door. They eyed the couple closely as Dan ushered Nellie toward a large potbellied stove, pulled a straight-backed chair toward it, and sat her down. As yet the two men had not caught sight of the silver shield on Dan's vest.

As he approached the desk, a tall, skinny man in

his mid-twenties stood up and faced him. The clerk's eyes widened as the shield arrested his attention. Dan caught a glimmer of fear on the man's face as his eyes darted toward the two unkempt loiterers.

"A room for you and the missus, mar—*sir?*" the clerk asked uneasily. He spun the register and handed Dan a pencil.

"It'll be two rooms, please," Dan said adjusting his gunbelt. "I found the lady half-frozen out on the trail. She will need a tub of hot water. Can you comply?"

"Oh, yes." The clerk managed a weak smile. "It will take about a half hour, but we can do it, sir."

Turning toward the door as he laid down the pencil, Dan spoke again as he purposely aimed the shield toward the two rowdies. "Livery stable close by?"

"Half a block north. Other side of the street," answered the obviously frightened clerk.

Dan held his position until he saw the eyes of the uglier one enlarge and his elbow gouge the other's ribs. The less ugly one then saw it for himself, said something Dan couldn't make out, and bolted out the door.

Nellie was settled in room six, awaiting the hot water, as Dan stepped out of number seven, directly across the hall. His room was street side, and he had spent the last five minutes observing a group of men down below, who were looking over the red roan. His plan was operating as intended. They recognized the horse and gear as belonging to one of the killers hired to dispose of Wilford Lewis.

As he descended the stairs, Dan was slipping into his Mackinaw when he saw the unkempt ugly man examining the register. Hearing the tall man's footsteps, he stepped away quickly.

Walking straight to him, Dan extended his right hand as he said, "I'm Marshal Wilford Lewis." The man tried to disguise the furtive look on his face with a blank smile, which immediately disappeared when Dan added, "But I guess you already know that."

Their hands never quite met. "Name's Lippy Norgren," he said evasively.

"Say, Norgren, where's the town marshal's office?"

"Boss, I tell yuh, I know it's Jim Rainey's roan. No question about it," the unsightly man said breathlessly. Kyle Waite bit the end off a cigar, fanned a match on his pant leg, and touched the flame to its tip.

"Stacks up to one thing." Waite's heavy voice filled the room. "Something dead sure went wrong." He ejected a string of curse words.

The door burst open. A short, stocky man wearing a badge entered the room noisily. "Kyle, what are we gonna do?" he puffed apprehensively.

"Keighley, you're going to learn to knock before you enter my office . . . or I'm going to knock your head." Waite could unnerve the average man with his menacing voice.

George Keighley wiped a nervous hand across his face and fingered his heavy mustache.

"I—I'm sorry, boss. I just—"

"Saldivar here just brought me the news." Waite rose from behind his desk, blew a cloud of smoke toward the ceiling. "We'll just play dumb. When he's convinced that everything is all right here, he'll be on his way."

Saldivar spoke up. "But, boss, we don't know how much he already knows. Maybe we better just put out his lights and drop him down one of the old mine shafts."

Waite's dark eyes touched Saldivar with a fierce look. "Sometimes I wonder about you, Alfredo. This bird was sent here from the government office in Raton. Who knows how many people he has talked to along the way? He doesn't show up there or report in at another U.S. marshal's office soon, they'll send the troops in."

Waite turned his huge frame toward Keighley. "Exactly what did that letter say?"

Keighley's face was blank. "What letter?"

Waite cursed. "You know what letter. The one this here marshal sent to Roy Sherman."

Keighley rubbed the back of his neck. "All it said was that someone who had been in here on the stage was slipped a note. They had carried it to the sheriff at Durango, and he had wired the marshal's office in Raton that Sherman had troubles and needed help. Went on to say that Marshal Lewis somebody would be here on the stage outta Durango on the fourteenth."

"Nuthin' about the mine?"

"No, Kyle. It said what I just told yuh. That's all."

Kyle Waite stared out the window. Snow was still sifting downward slowly. The room reeked with cigar smoke. "We're just gonna have to play it out, boys," he said, his back toward them.

"He's got a woman with him," Alfredo Saldivar said cautiously.

Kyle wheeled. "A woman?"

"Yep."

"Who is she?"

"Dunno. I think he told the clerk at the hotel that he picked her up on the trail."

"You *think*?" growled Waite.

"I was clear across the room, boss. I ain't sure."

"She may have been on that stage, boss," Keighley offered.

Kyle Waite took a deep breath. Setting his murky eyes on Welcome's "acting" marshal, he said, "You get back to your office, George. He'll come to you. Keep your wits about you and play it cool."

Keighley nodded and opened the door. "You'll hear from me."

When the door closed on Keighley's heels, Waite spoke to Saldivar. "What about the kid? Any change?"

"Don't think so, boss. Mrs. Bailey came and went out of the room a few times, but she knows she's supposed to let me'n' Lippy know if he stirs."

"You get back over there and—"

There was a loud knock at the door. "Boss! It's Lippy."

"It's open!" Waite's voice boomed.

Lippy Norgren's repulsive face appeared in the doorway. "Boss," he said, slamming the door, "you know thet there woman which come here with the marshal?"

"I didn't know about her till a moment ago. What is it?"

"She's that Bill Rice's wife."

Waite squinted his eyes in thought. "Bill Rice?"

"Yeah, you know. The rancher thet come lookin' fer thet Irishman . . . what's-his-name . . . uh, Dolan."

"Oh, yeah," said Waite indifferently. "Don't think I heard his name."

"We got problems," Norgren said gravely.

"So we ain't seen no Bill Rice. Who's to prove different?" asked the big dark man.

"Thet ain't my point," interjected Norgren. "She musta come here lookin' fer her husband. She's sure enough spilled the whole kettle of beans to that lawman. He knows there's two men come this way who have plumb disappeared. Thet there marshal is gonna git nosy."

Waite interlaced his fingers, palms forward, and cracked his knuckles. Biting hard on the cigar, he said, "This could get sticky."

"Boss, we shouldn'ta grabbed them ranchers who live so close around here," said Saldivar.

"Yeah, I know," Waite answered grudgingly. "But

with us having to kill those three fools who tried to escape, we were low on labor. If we ain't pulling gold out of that mine, we ain't getting rich."

Kyle Waite walked behind the desk and dropped his two hundred and sixty pound hulk into the leather-covered chair. Pulling open a drawer, he produced a half-empty whisky bottle. Releasing the cork, he lifted the bottle to his heavy lips and tilted it straight up. Lippy Norgren ran his tongue around his mouth while Alfredo Saldivar wiped away saliva with the back of his slimy hand.

After draining half the contents, Waite lowered the bottle, corked it, and returned same to the drawer. "We are just going to have to handle this situation a step at a time, boys."

Both men nodded.

"It might be a good idea for you boys to privately remind Mrs. Bailey that we're keeping her husband locked up as long as she's attending Louie Stokes. She's bound to run into that Rice woman, both of them being in the hotel. Put it on her hard. If she peeps a word, she's an instant widow."

A cold draft of air blanketed the town marshal's office when the door opened. George Keighley sat alone, next to the potbellied stove, which was stationed in the middle of the room. To the right of the door stood a worn oak desk, behind which hung a gunrack that bore two Winchester .44s and two shotguns. A stack of "wanted" posters lay in a slanted heap on the desk, along with a cup of cold black coffee, a coffee can half full of cigarette butts, and various scattered papers.

Keighley looked up to regard the man who stood framed in the doorway. His two-inch-high-heeled rider's boots put the top of his head six feet five inches from the floor. His wide-brimmed Stetson made him look even taller. The red and black checkered Mackinaw was fitted snugly over broad, muscular shoulders. A pair of twin Colt .45s were holstered on his narrow hips, thonged to solid thighs. His pale-blue eyes were set in a square, roughhewn face, extremely handsome. His fair skin was tanned and leathered by the sun and wind. The tall man's hair was medium blond, as was the heavy growth on his upper lip.

That was the external Dan Colt, rawhide tough, every inch a man. What lay beneath correlated with the exterior. There was in his eyes a marked glint of confidence and self-assurance, fringed with a hint of temper. All these commingled with a touch of warmth and human feeling.

Ducking his head as he passed through the framework, Dan closed the door and removed his hat. Charlie Lacy had told him the marshal's name was Roy Sherman.

"You Marshal Sherman?" queried Dan as he nonchalantly moved the open Mackinaw enough to expose the shield pinned to his vest.

Rising to his feet and forcing a smile, Keighley said, "No sir. He resigned and went back East to live."

Dan extended his hand. When the other man's hand met his grip, he squeezed down hard. "I'm Wilford Lewis. Work out of Raton."

"George Keighley," the same said, wincing.

"I assume you received the letter I sent to Sherman?"

"Uh . . . yes. Yes I did." Keighley felt tiny sweat beads form on his brow.

"What seems to be the trouble?" Dan asked as he removed the Mackinaw and draped it over an empty chair. Finding one near the stove, he sat down. Keighley found his again.

"Well, Mr. Lewis, I am a little puzzled about all of this," Keighley said, rubbing his heavy mustache.

"Meaning?"

"Your letter spoke of trouble Marshal Sherman was experiencing."

"Yes."

"Must be some kind of joke somebody's playing."

"Really?"

"You said something in your letter about a note being passed to a Fargo passenger and carried to the sheriff at Durango."

"Yep." Dan Colt's sky-colored eyes held Keighley in an invisible vise.

In an effort to break the spell the thick-bodied man pulled a cigarette from his shirt pocket and placed it between his lips. He had rolled it just prior to Dan's entrance. Leaning over, he gripped the wire-ring handle of a poker, which protruded from a small opening in the bottom of the stove. Touching the red-hot tip to the cigarette, he blew a cloud of smoke and replaced the poker in the fire.

"Got to be a joke," Keighley said flatly. "We ain't had no trouble since I been in office." He carelessly let his eyes meet Dan's, and the spell was on again. The man was reading him. *Get a grip on yourself*, he told himself. *This government dude is no dumbbell.*

"How long you been in office?" Dan probed. Dan *was* reading him. He was as nervous as a cockroach at a square dance.

"Little over three months," said Keighley, flicking ashes on the floor.

"That's strange," said Dan. "The note that went to Durango said that *Marshal Roy Sherman* was in trouble. That's why I wrote to *him*."

Dan was not sure that the note named Roy Sherman, but the faint odor of a rat was evident at this moment. He decided to pull a bluff and see if the rat would get scared enough to stick his nose out of the woodwork.

"Somebody made a mistake," George Keighley muttered uneasily.

"That note was written less than two weeks ago, sir," Dan rasped. "You mean that people in this town don't know who their own marshal is?"

The heavy-set man jumped to his feet. "Now, look here, Mr. Lewis, I don't know what you're driving at, but I don't like being questioned like a truant schoolboy!"

Dan Colt eased out of his chair and stood to full height. Towering over Keighley like a giant cedar over a sapling pinion, he said evenly, "Something stinks around here, George. The United States government sent me here to clean it up. I don't know what's going on, but I *will*. If I find out you're in on it, you better hunt yourself a big hole. I'm coming after you."

Keighley's face flushed with anger. Squaring his shoulders, he said, "I don't like being threatened."

Ignoring the hint of challenge, Dan asked, "What'd you do before they hired you as marshal here?"

"I, uh—uh . . . worked over at the Wells Fargo office."

George Keighley, being an outlaw, had little knowledge of how town marshals were hired. It was his notion that folks always hired a local man. The opposite was generally true. People liked to bring in a stranger, who would not be hindered in doing his sworn duty by family ties and long-established friendships. He felt safe in lying about the Wells Fargo office. Because of Ed Sorenson's contact with the travelers on the stagecoaches, one member of his family was always incarcerated and would be killed if he tipped his hand in the slightest. Sorenson would back up anything Keighley said.

Dan narrowed his eyes. "How long you work there?"

"Uh—six years. Yeah. Six years." He evaded Dan's gaze.

"What's the shotgunner's name on the Durango stage?"

Keighley's face drained white. Turning toward the stove, he pulled open the door. "Fire's going out." He tossed in a few chunks of wood and closed the door.

"I don't know what you're driving at, Lewis," he muttered. "You're trying to bluff me for some reason. You wouldn't know the shotgunner's name if I told you."

"Try me." Dan Colt's ice-blue eyes slammed him hard.

"Now, look here, mister, you ain't got no right—"

"The name," Dan retorted sharply.

"You're bluffing! You don't even know it!"

"You tell me what it is. Then I'll tell you what it is. Then we'll just walk over to the office. There are bound to be papers, delivery records, mailbag receipts with his signature on it. Maybe you'd rather name the driver. Let's hear it."

The fresh wood in the stove was now causing the fire to crackle.

George Keighley was trapped. It was take out Lewis or face the wrath of Kyle Waite for getting caught by him. Waite would be furious enough if Lewis was killed, but to let him learn of the mine operation, including the kidnaping and slavery, would kindle his hottest anger.

"Either name, George. I'm waiting."

Dan Colt had vast experience in facing men down. He saw the move in Keighley's eyes before the man's hand dropped toward his gun. With a quick step forward, Dan drove a hard fist into Keighley's nose. The muzzle of the gun had just cleared the top of the holster when fist met face. The revolver clattered to the floor as Keighley went down. As he rolled over, shaking his head, Dan toed the gun across the floor. It slid under the desk.

Dan had noticed a window sign lying on the desk upon entering. It read:

Marshal Out
Will Return Soon

While George Keighley was trying to clear his head, Dan threw the bolt on the door, stuck the sign in the window, and pulled the shade.

The thick-bodied man was rising to his feet and looking at the blood on his fingertips. It was running in a thin trickle from his left nostril.

Dan Colt closed in. He chopped him with a right cross, and Keighley went down again. Reaching down to the bottom of the hot stove, Dan grasped the wire-ring handle of the poker. The tip was red-hot.

The heavy-set man was rolling to his knees. Holding the poker in his right hand, Dan grabbed Keighley's collar, hoisted him to his feet, and slammed him against the closed door which led to the cells. Keighley was breathing hard. His eyes were slightly glazed.

Colt's left hand, filled with shirt, kept Keighley propped against the door. Slowly he lifted the bright-red tip of the poker and held it about two inches from the man's bleeding nose.

"Now, I want some straight answers, junior," Dan hissed through clenched teeth. "Somebody's got this town by the tail, and I've got a hunch you're part of it."

Keighley's eyes cleared and widened. "You wouldn't—"

"Wouldn't I?" Dan pushed the smoking tip a little closer.

"Now, look here, Lewis. This ain't no way for a lawman to act."

"How could you know? You're no lawman. You didn't work at the Fargo office either."

George Keighley sniffed blood, shook his head, and batted his eyes. "I ain't telling you nothing." A look of defiance formed on his face.

Dan pushed hard against the man's thick chest and edged the poker a little closer.

"Who you working for?"

"None of your bus—"

Dan nudged the hot metal into Keighley's heavy mustache. The hair curled and turned white with a slight hiss. He blinked in amazement as little wisps of smoke sifted upward. His countenance changed from defiance to cold fear.

"You're gonna kiss it, George, if you don't start talking *right now*."

"He'll kill me, Lewis," Keighley gasped. "If I tell you, I'm a dead man!"

"How does thirty years in prison sound, Georgie? Kidnaping draws a heavy penalty in Colorado. If anybody has died in your little game, mister, it'll be a *rope*!"

"Lewis, I'd rather face anything than Kyle Waite. He'd kill me an inch at a time!"

"Kyle Waite?"

Keighley's mind was spinning with fear. He had not realized what had come from his mouth till Dan repeated it. The frightened man closed his eyes and moaned.

"You give me the low-down on what's going on here, and this Kyle Waite will never know you told me. That's a promise, George."

Keighley swallowed hard. "How do I know I can trust you?"

"You don't," Dan retorted quickly. "But then, you aren't in a position to do much else, are you?"

"Lewis, when you make your arrests . . . will I get a break? Huh? If I help you, will I get a break?"

"I'll see what I can do," said Dan evenly.

"No! That's not good enough! I want your guarantee that you'll use your influence as U.S. marshal to—"

"I'll see what I can do," Dan repeated in the same tone.

"You promise you'll never let Waite know how you found out? Even if he goes to prison, he'll hound me down when he gets out. He'll kill me, Lewis!"

"I take it that none of your captives have been killed," Dan said, releasing his grip on Keighley's shirt.

"Three men were killed a few days ago, trying to escape. They also killed Roy Sherman. But their bodies can never be found. I didn't have anything to do with killing them, Lewis. That was Waite and his gunslicks. I don't think the law can ever pin it on them. There's no evidence."

George Keighley felt his mustache as he went back to his chair. The flow of blood from his nose had stopped.

Standing over him, Dan Colt asked, "What about Tom Dolan and Bill Rice?"

CHAPTER NINE

It had stopped snowing, and a break in the clouds revealed a portion of the sunset as Dan Colt emerged from the Welcome marshal's office. George Keighley had held nothing back. Dan now knew the whole situation. Tom Dolan and Bill Rice were laboring at the mine, along with eleven other men. The slaves were kept in an old bunkhouse out at the mine.

To keep any suspicion from being aroused, the gold was being transported to Denver in wagons rigged with false bottoms. Other items were carried visibly as a front. None of the Welcome gold ever appeared in any of the nearby towns. Food and supplies were transported in return from Denver.

The gang was holding townspeople as hostages in the old Fireside Hotel. The hostages were allowed no fires. Smoke from the chimneys would reveal to passersby that the old building with the boarded windows was in use. They kept warm by wrapping in blankets. Each day, Keighley had revealed, the hostages were rotated. The only exception was Howard Bailey. His wife was attending a youthful member of the gang who had been shot by a transient gunslinger and had not regained consciousness. Bailey would remain a hostage to ensure Mrs. Bailey's full cooperation. Other than Bailey, three hostages were held at all times. If any of the citizens of Welcome tried to make contact with someone passing through, one of the hostages would die. The same was true if anyone tried to leave town.

When Kyle Waite learned about the note which had been passed by some person in the town to a stagecoach passenger, he was furious. Choosing three men at random, he flogged them mercilessly. He warned that if it happened again, someone would die.

Dan Colt and George Keighley had an agreement. Keighley would continue to play his role. Colt would feign ignorance to the situation. He would remain in Welcome a few days under the guise of "investigating" the assertion of the smuggled note. Kyle Waite would feel safe as U.S. Marshal Wilford Lewis questioned the people. He had hostages.

Dan's plan was to alert the men of the town that he was aware of the circumstances. There was no way he could handle the whole gang alone.

He had noticed that the male citizens of the town wore their guns. Keighley advised him that none of them had ammunition. If the guns were not worn as usual, someone passing through might start asking questions. All the ammunition had been rounded up and was under guard, lock, and key at the gun shop, which had gone out of business shortly after the mines closed down.

Somehow the tall man would have to organize a surprise attack after he had successfully improvised a way to confiscate the ammunition. He must work fast. His "investigation" could not last too long without evoking Waite's suspicion.

There was also another reason for the haste. Lily Dolan. She had been through plenty already. He must expedite this thing and return Tom Dolan to her quickly.

As he angled across the snow-laden street toward the Mayflower Hotel, Dan Colt felt a slight tinge of guilt. He was no more a lawman than George Keighley. If the unsuspecting Keighley played his role out all the way to the end, the man posing as U.S. Marshal Wilford Lewis had absolutely no influence to assert on Keighley's behalf.

George Keighley nervously opened the door of the Empire Saloon, which was located directly across the street from the Fireside Hotel. Passing by the dust-covered bar, he weaved his way through the maze of dusty tables, laden with chairs, flipped seat-downward.

"It's about time, George," a voice said from a corner in the gathering darkness. "The boss was gettin' worried."

Keighley paused before knocking on the office door and looked toward the voice. At the same moment Kyle Waite's sentinel snapped a match with a thumbnail and raised the flame to a cigarette. The momentary flare revealed the man's face.

"He's a smart lawman, Rex," Keighley replied, attempting a tone of self-confidence. "Took some real talking to convince him that nothing's going on here."

"For the sake of your hide I hope you did it," replied the sentinel icily.

Keighley knocked on the door. A heavy voice from within bade him open it.

As George Keighley closed the door behind him, Kyle Waite boomed, "Took you long enough, George!" A lantern was burning on a small table next to Kyle Waite's desk.

Removing his hat and guiding it in circles over his fingertips, Keighley gave a wordy explanation of how he had masterfully overcome the curiosity of the United States marshal and fully convinced him that there was nothing shady going on in Welcome.

Kyle reared back in his chair and folded his massive arms. "So when's he leaving?"

Keighley rubbed his mustache. "Well, he says that

since the sending of the note is on record at his office, he will have to talk to the townspeople and do some investigating."

Waite squinted and eyed Keighley's upper lip. "What'd you do to your mustache? Looks like you tried to eat the live end of a seegar."

"Oh, yeah," Keighley said smiling, "you know I sometimes light my smokes with the stove poker? Well, I wasn't watching what I was doing and *I missed*!" He laughed nervously.

"Lewis say how long he'd be carrying on this here investigation?"

"He thinks two, three days. How ever long it takes to chalk up enough satisfactory answers from the people."

Waite swore. "Why should it take that long to talk to a handful of people?"

"I dunno, Kyle," Keighley said, wiping his palms on his pants.

"If he wasn't a government man, I'd bore him full of holes and hang his hide from the nearest tree!" roared Waite, banging his giant fist on the desk.

A tin cup, half full of cold coffee, jumped with the impact and clattered to the floor. George Keighley bent over, picked it up, and replaced it on the desk.

"What about the stage?" Waite asked, reaching in a desk drawer and lifting out a cigar.

"Huh?" George's face blanched. He had forgotten to ask Wilford Lewis about the Wells Fargo stagecoach and why he had ridden into town on the roan. Waite's hard-featured face was dreadful in the dim light of the lantern. "I . . . uh . . . well, I forgot about that, boss. I'm sor—"

"Looks like I picked the wrong man for that marshal's job, George. You losin' your brains in your old age?"

"No, sir, I . . . I just got so wrapped up trying to steer his thinking that it slipped my mind."

"You talk to him, George. I want you standing right there by nine o'clock in the morning with some answers about that stage. Understand?"

"Yes, sir. I'll have the information for you."

A knock at the door relieved the tension.

"Come in!" Waite roared.

One of Waite's lieutenants had come to give a report concerning the mine. George Keighley excused himself and groped his way in the darkness toward the outside door of the closed-down saloon.

As Dan Colt passed the desk in the lobby of the Mayflower, he pulled off the Mackinaw. The skinny desk clerk gave him a brief smile. The tall man paused, returning the smile, and said, "Is Mrs. Rice in her room?"

"No, sir," the clerk replied. "She is in room number one just at the top of the stairs."

Dan smelled the aroma of cooked food coming from the dining room. His neglected stomach immediately seized the opportunity to register a complaint.

"She's visiting with Mrs. Bailey," the clerk continued. "Just rap on the door."

As he ascended the stairs, Dan took note of the two scruffy-looking men who sat in the horsehair chairs. They were not the same ones as were posted earlier.

Stopping at the door with a big numeral one painted on the cross panel, he rapped lightly. A gray-haired matronly woman opened the door a few inches. Her face was grim until she spied the shield on his vest. A broad smile crept across her face. "Hello, Marshal Lewis. I'm Flora Bailey. I'll bet you're looking for Nellie."

"Yes, ma'am," Dan answered, removing his hat.

His ears picked up the familiar swish of feminine attire as Nellie Rice approached the door. When it came all the way open, Dan saw the young man in the bed. His head was heavily bandaged. His eyes were closed.

Nellie smiled as she looked up at the tall man.

"Did you get thawed out?" he asked warmly.

"Uh-huh. But I think I've caught cold." There was a definite nasal tone to her speech. Her nose was red. "Mrs. Bailey has given me some of her home remedy."

"It will have her good as new in a couple days," chimed Flora Bailey.

"May I take you to dinner?" Dan asked politely.

Nellie curtsied. "I would be delighted, Marshal Lewis," she said, touching a hanky to her nose. Turning to the matronly woman, she said, "Thank you for the company, Mrs. Bailey. I'll see you later."

"Oh," gasped Mrs. Bailey, "don't forget your medicine. As she spoke, she walked to a chest of drawers and lifted a dark-colored bottle. Handing it to Nellie, she said, "Take a good dose before going to bed, my dear. You will feel worlds better by morning."

As they walked down the hall toward their respective rooms, Dan whispered, "I've got good news. Bill is alive. So is Tom."

Nellie's hand flew to her mouth as tears filled her eyes. "Oh, thank God!" she whispered. *"Thank God!"*

As Dan Colt and Nellie Rice ate supper in the hotel dining room, the two unshaven Waite henchmen eyed them warily from the lobby.

A man and a woman occupied a table on the other side of the room. Otherwise the dining room was empty. A masculine-looking woman was both cook and waitress. She had retired to the kitchen. Keeping his voice low, Dan told Nellie of his confrontation with George Keighley and of the subsequent agreement. He explained his plan in detail.

She listened intently until he had finished. "Now I understand why—" The manly woman had emerged through the kitchen door and was approaching the table with a steaming coffeepot.

"More coffee?" she asked in a husky voice.

"Please," Nellie said, lifting her cup.

"You, Marshal?" she asked, already pouring it into his cup.

"Sure," Dan grinned.

The woman was clothed in a wool dress but looked like she would be more at home in overalls. Dan was sure he could detect heavy biceps underneath the tight-fitting sleeves. She had shoulders like a logger, a neck like a wrestler, and the hands of a corn shucker. Her dark hair was pulled straight back and rolled neatly in a bun. Her jaw was square, with lines of determination. Dan figured she stood nearly six feet tall and would weigh in at about one eighty. Her face was socketed with dark, flinty eyes.

"The meal all right?" she asked, looking straight at Dan.

"Sure is, Miss—"

"Missus," she said reprovingly. "He was no good. Drunk hisself into the grave."

"Oh," said Dan, nonplussed.

"Need anything else, jist holler."

Dan nodded. Annie turned, paused momentarily at the other occupied table, then disappeared into the kitchen.

Nellie blew on her coffee, trying to suppress a burst of laughter.

Dan smiled and shook his head. "That old girl could go bear huntin' with a switch!" He sipped the hot coffee. "You were saying something about understanding?"

"Oh. Yes. I was thinking about Mrs. Bailey. We met in the hallway this afternoon. She was very evasive on any subject pertaining to the town. Twice, when I asked about her husband, I saw tears in her eyes. She would only say that he was not home right now. That's what I meant. Now I understand."

Nellie placed her cup in the saucer. Dan saw a compassionate look in her eyes. "Dan, that boy up there in the bed. Some professional gunfighter started a ruckus here a few days ago and shot him."

"Is he gonna make it?" Dan asked with concern.

"There's no way of knowing yet."

"They ought to get him to a doctor."

"Mrs. Bailey said Doc Farley was here nearly three days with him. He's the doctor in Ouray."

"Is the boy from Welcome?"

"I—I really don't know," Nellie said, dabbing a napkin at her lips.

"Keighley told me he was part of the gang."

"But, Dan, he's so young. Probably not over eighteen."

"Head wound, huh?"

"Yes. The bullet creased his skull. He's been unconscious ever since. How could a kid like that get mixed up with the gang?"

"Maybe they were trying to hire this gunslinger like they hired your husband and Tom Dolan."

"Oh." Nellie folded her napkin and laid it beside her plate. Looking up at him, she said, "Dan, how can we ever repay you for what you're doing? You don't even know us."

"It will be payment enough to see you and Bill together again and to know the Dolan family is reunited."

"But you must have been headed somewhere on your way to something, when the stagecoach got robbed." Nellie's eyes were searching Dan's face.

"It's a long story, ma'am. To keep it short, I was on my way north, looking for my brother." He finished his coffee and set the cup down.

"Your brother? Is he as charming as you?"

Dan Colt's face flushed slightly. "Don't know, ma'am."

"You're just being modest," she said with a sly smile. "Is he older or younger than you?"

"One of us has a few minutes over the other, but I don't know which."

Nellie's eyes widened. "Your *twin*? Oh, that's nice! I'll bet you two are very close."

"Well, not exactly. I—"

"Are you identical?"

"Yes, ma'am." Dan cleared his throat.

"Must be a terrible thing for the ladies . . . trying to choose—" Nellie's face twisted. She reached for her hanky and sneezed into it, sniffed, and sneezed again.

"I think we'd better get you upstairs so you can load up on Mrs. Bailey's Indian River medicine and get to bed," Dan said with a broad smile. "I'll fill you in on my past later."

After bidding Nellie good night at her door, Dan stepped across the hall and entered his own room. Leaving the door open to make use of the light from the hallway, he crossed the room to the dresser. Running his fingers lightly over the top, he found a match. Lifting the glass chimney from the coal oil lamp, he thumbed the match and touched the flame to the wick. After adjusting the wick, he replaced the chimney and retraced his steps to close the door.

As he pushed the door shut, something caught his eye on the floor. It was a folded sheet of paper. Someone had slipped it under the door. He turned the key in the lock, stooped, and picked up the paper. Moving toward the lantern, Dan unfolded the sheet and angled it toward the light. It had been printed carefully.

Marshal Lewis—
We are being held prisoners in our own town by

> Kyle Waite and his gang. They have reopened the number 3 mine and are using the town as a trap to capture men who are passing through. They force them to work in the mine.
>
> Waite's office is in the back of the Empire Saloon. Hostages are being held in the Fireside Hotel. George K. is not our marshal. We are not sure what happened to Marshal Sherman. We think they killed him.
>
> Someone will be killed if Waite finds out you received this note. PLEASE HELP US!

After rereading the message, Dan tilted a corner of the paper into the opening at the top of the glass chimney. He held it there until the paper turned brown, curled upward, and burst into flame. Changing hands and turning the note in circles, he let it burn totally.

Dan lay in the darkness for some time before dropping off to sleep. He thought of Nellie's relief in learning that her husband was alive. He wished that Lily could know about Tom. He satisfied himself with the thought that no matter what it took, within a couple of days Tom would be home. By the tone of the note that was shoved under his door, he felt that the people would be ready to rally behind him.

His thoughts turned to Dave Sundeen. Where was he by now? He reflected on the five months he had spent in Yuma Territorial Prison because he had been mistaken for his outlaw twin. The florid face of Logan Tanner floated into his mind. The town marshal of Holbrook, Arizona, had sent him off to Yuma, not believing a word about a twin brother. Dan remembered the promise he had made to himself. He would capture Dave, walk him into Tanner's office, and *rub their noses together*.

Shedding his mind of all these things, he thought of Mary. Beautiful, sweet, loving Mary. How complete she had made his life. How empty he had been before he met her. His life had been a shiftless, aimless void. He had saddled through the West, riding from town to town. Here, a job as hired gun. There, tracking an outlaw for the bounty. Restless and hollow inside, he had stayed on the move.

Then came that day in Wichita. Suddenly there was Mary. Her eyes were aglow with vibrant life. The sunlight danced on her dark hair.

If ever a man fell in love at first sight, it was Daniel Colt.

He had avenged her death. Each of her three killers left this life violently. But that fact could never ease his loneliness. With Mary gone, he was back where he started, riding from town to town. Even when he finally captured Dave and cleared his name, the solitary wilderness inside him would still be there. He had one consolation. At least he had her memory . . .

CHAPTER TEN

Morning came with a clear blue sky and the optimism generated by radiant sunlight. The world looked bright and clean.

After a generous breakfast cooked and served by Annie Rankin, Dan Colt trudged through the snow toward the livery stable. By now the gang had heard from George Keighley. It was time to unnerve them by being seen riding out of town. He would head south, then veer east and take a look at the operation. George Keighley had reluctantly described the location of the mine.

Astride the roan, he headed south through town. As he approached the marshal's office, George Keighley emerged from the door and waved. At first Dan thought it was a simple gesture of acknowledging his presence. The thought was quelled when Keighley lifted his voice and said, "Lewis! I need to see you."

Swinging the gelding to the hitching rail, Dan dismounted. Keighley's eyes were puffy. Dan figured the man had probably spent a sleepless night.

"Where you goin'?" Keighley asked, dangling a cigarette from the corner of his mouth.

"For a little ride," Dan answered in an unfriendly tone.

"You go ridin' around, and Waite will get nervous."

"Mm-hmm. That's exactly what I want. When they get strung out tight, they make mistakes."

Dan noticed the shorter man's nose was also swollen. He had shaved off the mustache. "What did you want to see me about?"

"Waite wants—"

Keighley's attention was drawn to the south end of the snow-covered street. Six riders were moving toward them slowly. The few people on the street eyed them cautiously.

"Gunslingers," said Dan.

"Waite's new men," replied George Keighley solemnly. "Replacements for the ones that hot-shot gunslick killed in the saloon a few days ago. One in the lead is the honcho that Waite sent to Socorro to hire them."

"You're telling me that one man gunned down *five* of Waite's men?" Dan asked, his blond eyebrows arched.

"Yep. He left four men dead and the kid unconscious with a crease in his skull. He hasn't come around yet. Still out. They're keeping him over there in the Mayflower."

"What's this fella's name?"

"Louie Stokes. He's only eighteen or so."

"No, I mean the gunslinger."

"Don't know. They had him closed in all private like. Was gonna stick him in the mine. Only ones that got a look at his face are dead. 'Cept Louie."

The six riders pulled up to the hitching rail where Dan Colt and George Keighley stood. Three of them swung around the roan while the remaining three closed in on the short side. The rider who dismounted on the right side of the roan seemed irritated. He began cursing loudly. His sudden outburst startled the animal. Its ears pricked upward, eyes widening. The man bellowed again. The roan sidestepped nervously, bumping his rump against the horse on the other side, then rebounded, slamming the rider hard against his own horse.

The man cursed and drove a fist into the roan's flank. Dan bounded over the rail and dived between the horses. His full weight caught the gunslinger, driving him to the rear of the frightened animals and down in the street. Both men rolled in the snow, gaining their feet.

Fury rode Colt's face. "That's no way to treat a horse, mister. Especially another man's."

"Stupid beast tried to crush me," snapped the man, spitting snow from his mouth.

"He wouldn't have moved a muscle if you hadn't shot off your mouth. You're the one that's stupid!" Dan's eyes flashed.

The rider lunged for him, swinging wildly. The agile Colt pumped a right, then a left, dropping him to his back. He rolled over, shaking his head. Dan waited till he straightened up, then moved in. The tall man chopped him viciously with a left hook, followed it with a heavy right under the heart, and snapped a hard left cross. The rider staggered sideways and fell face down in the snow.

Brushing snow from his clothes, Dan stepped to the roan and stroked its nose. "It's all right, boy. He won't do that again."

Two of the riders went to the aid of their fallen comrade. The others eyed Dan with a mixture of awe and contempt. His heavy Mackinaw was buttoned. No one had seen the badge pinned to his vest.

The lead man spoke to George Keighley. "Who's the long dude, George?"

Before Keighley could answer, Dan said, "Wilford Lewis. And you are—"

"Tate Landry," the man replied coldly.

Turning to Keighley, Dan said, "If you've got business with Landry, I can see you later."

"Uh, no," Keighley said quickly. "I gotta talk to you right now. Go on into the office."

Dan moved toward the door. He heard Keighley

say, "Tate, which one of these boys is the new bartender?"

"Wrigley, here," answered Landry, pointing.

Addressing Wrigley, George pointed up the street. "The Rockaway Saloon. Can't miss it. Fella there called Ben Bleier. He'll show you around."

Wrigley nodded, mounted up.

"Might as well take the rest right on over to Kyle, Tate," Keighley said. "He'll want to give them the old break-in speech."

Dan opened the office door and looked over his shoulder. His latest opponent was now up on wobbly legs, shaking his snow-covered head. Keighley and Tate exchanged more words as Dan entered the office, leaving the door open. Presently Keighley followed, closing the door.

"Waite wants to know about the stagecoach, Lewis," George said, flopping his hat on the desk.

"What stagecoach?" Dan asked, placing his hat on a chair.

"The one you took out of Durango."

"It was Waite's killers, eh?"

"Yes," Keighley responded, looking at the floor.

"I don't cotton to him planning my demise," Dan said, features stiff.

Keighley cleared his throat, wiped his hand over his bare upper lip. "Guess I can't blame you for feelin' that way. So what happened?"

Dan Colt weaved a believable story, killing off some of the attackers, leaving a question as to the others. He pitched the stagecoach over the cliff and invented a leap to safety for the intended victim.

"How about the driver . . . the shotgunner?" Keighley queried.

"They shot the gunner. Driver tried to jump clear. Split his head open on a rock."

"So you grabbed the roan and rode on in."

"Yep." The tall man retrieved his hat, placed it on his head. "That all you need?"

Before Keighley could answer, a gun roared just outside the door. Springing toward the door, Dan flung it open. The man he had left lying in the street earlier was standing over the roan. The gelding was lying on its side, kicking stiffly. Blood was spewing from the bullet hole between its eyes.

Dan charged through the door. The man was holding a smoking Colt .45. Flicking a glance at Dan, he raised the gun and pulled the trigger. He was too late. The tall man had palmed both .45s and fired first. Both bullets tore into his chest. He fell backward, dropping the gun. Still alive, he rolled over and raised to his knees. After a single spasm, he coughed and fell motionless. A crimson stream soaked into the snow, turning it red, then almost black.

The tall man holstered his guns and turned his attention to the horse. The animal lay motionless, a pool of blood in the snow next to its head. Dan was glad he had left his black gelding with Lily Dolan.

A crowd was gathering. He spoke to George Keighley. "I'm going to buy another horse. The hostler will bring the bill to you. He better be paid by the time I get back."

Keighley nodded. Dan Colt would get no argument from him. He was sure Waite would pay for the horse rather than stir up trouble with the law. The outlaw leader was eager only to get the U.S. marshal out of Welcome.

Dan looked into the eyes of the collecting crowd. The strain of Welcome's bondage was evident in their pinched faces. He wanted to say something to give them hope . . . just a glint of encouragement. He could think of nothing. Now was not the time.

It was just before nine o'clock when George Keighley entered the door of the Empire Saloon. He could not afford to be late. Kyle Waite was not a patient man. Keighley paused for a few seconds in the doorway, watching Dan Colt ride a large bay gelding southward. As he edged out of town, concealed eyes followed him until the bay carried him out of sight. Immediately a runner made hasty tracks toward the Empire.

The tall blond man squinted his weather-tempered eyes against the sun glare as he veered the bay off the road. The snow clung to the giant trees and blanketed the earth in a coverlet of dazzling white. Halting among the trees, he scanned his back trail. If anyone was following, they were laying back out of sight. He would be easily tracked in the snow, but he doubted that anyone would follow. Should he spot them, it would only arouse his suspicion. They would do nothing to delay his departure.

Spurring the gelding lightly, he guided it through the trees. A chipmunk scurried across his path and darted up a thick-trunked pine. Circling south of town, he angled eastward in the direction of the mine.

This was a wild and lonely country. Mountain peaks on all sides seemed to stretch forever. Each one lifted its snow-capped head as if to look down on the others. A man could travel for miles upon miles in these rugged mountains and never see another human being.

Dan found himself climbing higher. In some places the going was rough. At one point he had to dismount and lead the horse through a spill of timber and broken rock. The snow was deep enough to brush the gelding's belly. Tree branches and brush snapped at man and beast as they shouldered through the narrow spill.

Mounting again as he topped out on a rocky ridge, Dan lifted his gaze in time to see a small herd of deer melt into the shadows just ahead. As he reached the same trees where the deer had been moments before, he reined in and studied his back trail. Nothing moved. Apparently no one was following.

Time passed slowly. The sun climbed higher in its solitary domain. The air was growing warmer, and Dan noticed water beginning to drip from the trees. It was getting close enough to spring for even this high country to feel the warm rays of the sun.

Soon horse and rider were making their way off a narrow shelf, following a natural trail down the side of a mountain. Descending into a shallow draw, Dan pulled the horse to a halt. The primeval silence was suddenly broken by a sharp, cracking sound. It was coming from somewhere below him, to his left. The sound was steady and even. As he moved closer, he recognized the banging of a single jack. *The mine!*

In his travels Dan Colt had spent some time in mining camps. The steady hammering of the single jack was a familiar sound.

The mine would be carefully guarded. He must not be seen. Cautiously he dismounted, tying the bay to a tree. Crouching low, he plodded through the snow in the direction of the heavy sound. Presently the entire camp came into view over a snow-laden ridge of boulders. It lay about a hundred feet below. Dan hunkered down. About forty feet to the right of the yawning hole in the side of the mountain was the hoist-house. Off to the left the other buildings were huddled together. The long string of windows in the bunkhouse reflected the glare of the sun off the snow. There was a thin thread of smoke climbing skyward from the rusty old chimney on the cookshack.

Someone had shoveled the snow off the narrow-gauge trolley track which ran in circular fashion from the hoist-house into the dark shaft.

Three guards were visible. The cook had momentarily opened the cookshack door to toss out a dishpan of soapy water. Once he disappeared back into the shack, Dan could only see the three men who bore Winchesters. He assumed the rest of the camp would be the captive workers, and they would be down in the mine. He wondered that there were not more than three guards. Of course there would be some down in the mine, but certainly there must be others in the area who were not visible to him.

Checking the area around him, Dan saw no movement. He cast a quick glance toward the bay, which stood patiently beneath the dripping tree. He noted that the saddle was now shining with melted snow from the tree limbs.

Swinging his gaze back toward the mining camp below, he looked just in time to see a mule team emerging from the dark shaft, pulling a trolley car full of ore. They were led by a man who walked with a slight limp. Following the trolley car was a man bearing a Winchester rifle, who also wore a lamp-cap. The procession was slowly making its way to the hoist-house. The single jack continued to hammer out its monotonous tune.

About the time the trolley car reached the hoist-house, another one appeared, moving at the same slow pace. This one also was followed by an armed guard. It was led by an elderly man.

Dan thought of Tom Dolan and Bill Rice. By this time their spirits were probably at a low ebb. The thing to do now was to get back to town and rally the people, one by one. Once they had overtaken the gang in town, the overpowering of the guards here at the mine would be relatively simple.

The nervous nicker of the bay brought the tall man's attention around. Standing about thirty feet to his left was a dark-eyed man with a Winchester leveled at his chest. A wicked grin spread across his bearded face.

"Lookin' fer somethin', mister?"

Slowly Colt stood up, looking the man dead in the eye.

"How 'bout reachin' fer a piece of blue, mister?"

Dan raised his hands shoulder high. The man cautiously walked closer. Spitting a brown stream of tobacco juice from the side of his mouth, he snarled, "Nosin' around where you ain't got no business, ain'tcha?"

"I'm a United States marshal," Dan said evenly. "You could do a prison stretch just for holding a gun on me. I'm here to investigate this operation, and if you detain me with that gun, you are obstructing justice. Could go mighty bad for you."

"Not if I blow yer stinkin' head off," the bearded rifleman said, casually spitting another brown stream. "Besides, I don't see no badge."

"It's on my vest, under the coat."

"Why don't we just meander down to the mine. We'll have the boss take a look at you. He'll decide what to do."

It was apparent to Dan that Kyle Waite had kept the fact of the presence of Marshal Wilford Lewis in Welcome from his men at the mine. He probably had figured to get shed of the lawman without disturbing things.

"Let's go," said the man, motioning with the muzzle.

Dan noted that the man wore heavy gloves. His forefinger was placed alongside the trigger but was not curled around it. There was no question he could draw and fire before his assailant could pull the trigger. But to do so would alert the other guards. He must find a way to disarm him without noise.

"Can I get my horse?" Dan asked, nodding toward the bay.

"I'll send somebody after him," the man said roughly. "Now let's git down to the camp."

Dan shrugged his shoulders. "All right. Which way?"

Gesturing with the muzzle again, the bearded man pointed to Dan's right. "Thetaway. Now, git!"

Keeping his hands at shoulder level, the man posing as Marshal Wilford Lewis began to walk through the snow. There seemed to be a path which led through a heavy stand of pine trees. Dan assumed that it would lead down the grade to the mine. The man holding the gun on him must have come from another direction. There were no footprints in the snow ahead.

As they entered the trees, Dan took note that the branches were hanging low. The warmth of the sun had not filtered into the shadowed density of the big pines. The branches were stiff with cold and, if bent back hard, would recoil with great force. Pine needles striking the face violently would produce excruciating pain.

With his hands at shoulder height, they were in a perfect position to grasp the branches. They walked for several minutes. Dan casually brushed at the heavy branches, bobbing and weaving his way through. His assailant was keeping step just one pace behind him. Several times when Dan broke his stride, ducking branches, the rifle muzzle prodded his back. He was glad the man was following so close. The banging of the single jack echoed through the hills.

Just ahead Dan saw a slight ledge in the path. It would be about a two-feet drop. Heavy branches hovered low. Making sure the man was close on his heels, he made as if he was using a branch to steady himself as he stepped over the ledge. He feigned a slight forward stumble, which allowed him to spring the branch. Twisting so he would see, he timed it perfectly. The heavy branch recoiled fiercely, striking the man square in the face. Pine needles pierced his eyes.

Dan was on him like a cat. The rifle fell to the snow. The man started to yell. Dan jammed snow in his mouth. He fought furiously, trying desperately to cry out.

The two men rolled in the snow. Kyle Waite's guard blinked against his smarting eyes, doing his best to fight free of the muscular Dan Colt. Spitting snow, the bearded man was able to ejaculate a slight cry. Dan hit him hard with a balled fist. The man slumped slightly but opened his mouth again to shout.

Dan hit him again, but they were tumbling on a steep grade, writhing in two-feet-deep snow, and he could not hit him hard enough to knock him out.

As they rolled further, the bearded man found a short piece of tree limb which had lodged in the snow. It was about three feet long and heavy. Dan was trying to gain his balance when the limb caught him on the right cheekbone. Lights flashed in his head as he felt his back hit the snow. The earth was spinning furiously. He could hear his assailant breathing heavily.

The club came down hard but buried itself harmlessly in the snow. Dan shook his head, and the earth stopped spinning just as the man stood over him, raising the club again.

Dan rolled sideways. When the heavy branch struck the snow where his head had been one second before, he grasped the man's legs and toppled him. If the bearded man had not been gasping so hard for breath, he would have cried out. Dan knew he could not keep him from yelling much longer. He pounced on the man, who was now wheezing. His eyes were bulging. His face was purple. Dan was about to hit him again when suddenly his opponent exhaled one long breath and went limp. His eyes bulged sightlessly. He was dead.

Dan stood over him for a long moment. *Must have been his heart,* he thought to himself.

CHAPTER ELEVEN

Dan Colt knew it would not be long until some of the other guards would come looking for their friend. There was no way he could obliterate the trail they had left. Nor could he disguise the evident signs of struggle. The best thing for him to do was to get out of there quickly.

Within a few minutes he had ascended back to the bay and squared himself on the wet saddle. It made no difference now. He was soaked anyway. Slipping the twin Colts from their holsters, he rubbed off the snow and freed the cylinders. They needed to be in perfect working order at all times.

As he moved the gelding out from under the trees, Dan spotted the footprints of the bearded man coming from higher up, along the edge of the precipice which overlooked the mining camp.

Nudging the horse slightly with his knees, he followed the footprints as they worked away from the edge of the precipice and made their way upward. Dan soon found himself deep in the trees at a point which would be directly over the mine.

The footprints led to a squared wooden apparatus, which lay adjacent to the ground. It would not be noticeable, except that the man had come through it and dislodged the snow which had covered it. Stepping from the saddle, Dan approached it. He could hear the sledging of the mine tools as they echoed in the shaft. This was a secret entrance, or exit. For some unknown reason the bearded man had climbed up here and had spotted Dan below, observing the camp. Apparently he had not told anyone he was climbing out. No one, at least, had followed.

It was past noon when Dan rode back into Welcome. Melted snow was dripping from the roofs. A few people mingled on the streets. One by one Dan caught their attention as he rode slowly toward the livery stable.

A big shaggy dog stepped off the board sidewalk, looked up at the tall man, and walked alongside the bay, wagging his tail.

As he passed the marshal's office, Dan saw George Keighley peering through the window. He wondered if Kyle Waite was ever going to show himself while Marshal Wilford Lewis was on the scene.

He learned from the hostler that he, indeed, had been paid by George Keighley for the bay. Crossing the lobby of the hotel, he felt the eyes of the two original guards follow him up the stairs. As he passed room number one, the door was closed. He wondered if Nellie Rice was keeping Mrs. Bailey company. He thought about the wounded boy and wondered if he had regained consciousness.

Entering his room, he fumbled through the saddlebags, laying out dry clothing. After changing clothes, he paused and looked at himself in the mirror. His right cheekbone was swollen and caked with dried blood. This, added to the claw marks from the wolf on his left temple and forehead, gave him the appearance of having come out second in a face-disfiguring contest.

He pulled the door shut behind him and turned the key. Stepping across the hall, he knocked lightly on Nellie's door. There was no answer. *She must be with Mrs. Bailey,* he thought.

Dan Colt's plan was to begin with Ed Sorenson, the Wells Fargo agent. Sorenson seemed to be a leader in

Welcome. If he could get the Fargo man convinced the Kyle Waite's gang could be overcome, he would be the spark to fire the revolt.

As he descended the stairs, one of Waite's grizzled guards was at the lobby door, looking out through the window. The other one watched the tall man warily as he crossed the lobby toward the door. The man blocking the door turned slowly as Dan approached. His jaw was set hard, and his eyes flashed a look of defiance. Halting briefly, Dan looked down at the shorter man. "Move your tail, or I'll break your neck, sonny."

The unkempt man eyed Dan's bloody cheekbone. "What happened to the other fella, Marshal?"

"The same thing that's going to happen to you, if I have to wait two more seconds," Dan said heavily.

Locking his eyes with those of the tall man, he slid sideways. Dan opened the door and was immediately outside, heading for the Wells Fargo office.

As he passed the old tobacco shop, he noted the wooden cigar-store Indian standing outside the door. He had never seen one quite like it. Instead of a full headdress, this one wore a derby hat. Life size, it stood nearly six feet tall.

As he passed the Buffalo Cafe, he thought of Slim Withers. Charlie Lacy had spoken of him. He was on Dan's list of men to contact.

Continuing along the snow-covered boardwalk, he heard footsteps behind him. Casting a look over his shoulder, he saw two of Waite's henchmen following at a distance of about fifty feet. Dan reached the Wells Fargo door, opened it, stepped inside, and closed the door behind him. A large bald-headed man was seated near a potbellied stove. Dan judged him to be in his mid-fifties.

"Ed Sorenson?" Dan asked as the man stood up.

"Yes, sir," replied Sorenson, extending his hand. "And you're Marshal Lewis?"

Dan nodded, scanning the room. Sorenson was alone. "I want to talk to you," Dan said quietly.

Sorenson looked nervously over the tall man's shoulder. At the same moment the door opened, and Dan turned to see the two men enter who had been following him. The second man closed the door. Sorenson cleared his throat uneasily.

"You gentlemen have business in here?" Dan asked with his face like granite.

"We just came in to rest awhile," the first one answered coldly.

"You can get a bed at the hotel," Dan snapped, his eyes flashing.

"We'd rather rest right here," the man retorted.

Dan Colt unbuttoned his coat, pulling it open, exposing the badge. "I'm United States Marshal Wilford Lewis, mister. I have business with Mister Sorenson of official nature. Now, since you gentlemen have already established that you have no business here, you just move out. *Now*."

The second man spoke up. "Let's go, Joe. We don't want to rile the marshal."

Joe nodded and turned toward the door as the other man opened it. Pausing in the doorway, Joe looked at the agent and said with a half smile, "How's your wife, Ed? She feeling all right?"

Sorenson got the message. Dan understood it but feigned ignorance.

"She's fine," Sorenson answered weakly.

"That's nice," said Joe and closed the door.

Ed Sorenson produced a large red handkerchief and mopped his moistened brow. "Marshal, I can't talk to you. Don't ask me to explain it. Please just accept my apology and let me be."

Swinging a round-backed wooden chair next to the one where Sorenson had been sitting, Dan lowered himself onto it. "Sit down, Mr. Sorenson. You don't have to explain it. I already know all about it."

The bald man's jaw slacked. "You do?" He mopped his brow again.

"Yep."

"How?"

"I'll explain that later. Right now there isn't time."

"You're sure you know—"

"I've got the whole picture," Dan replied, placing his right calf on his left knee. "I know about Kyle Waite and his skunks treeing this town. I know they have all of you scared spitless. They murdered your marshal and stuck Keighley in his place."

Sorenson was sitting in his chair, facing Dan Colt. He had been hunched over slightly, looking into the tall man's pale blue eyes. At Dan's last statement, he straightened up, eyes widened. "So they *did* kill him?"

"Yessir."

"None of us knew for sure, but we feared as much." Sorenson shook his head.

"We can't talk long, or they *will* suspect something," said Dan. "I looked the mine over this morning. Couldn't see much. I was stationed on a ledge up above it."

He dropped his right foot to the floor again. "I've got a plan, Mister Sorenson. I know about the ammunition locked up in the gun shop. If we can get all the men to join together, we can overtake this bunch of cutthroats and free the town."

Sorenson mopped his forehead again. "I don't know, Marshal. They've got us scared to make a move. I assume you know that they keep a number of us locked up in the old Fireside Hotel at all times."

Dan nodded.

"If we so much as *look* like we are going to buck them or expose them, they'll start killing us. I guess you understood Joe Clary's question about my wife."

"Mm-hmm," Dan hummed with expression.

"If we made some mistake in pulling it off, Marshal, who knows how many of us they'd kill? If we were not one hundred percent successful, it would be a bloody massacre."

"We can do it if all the men will cooperate," said Dan with a note of optimism.

"I see at least three major problems, Marshal," Ed said, rubbing his jaw.

Dan waited.

"Kyle Waite keeps the key to the gun shop himself. There is no way to break in. The place is well fortified. Has been a gun shop from the beginning. Windows are barred. There's no back door. The one door is solid oak, two inches thick. How we gonna get to the ammunition?"

Dan smiled. "I've got a hammerlock on George Keighley. With a little pressure in the right place, he will find a way to relieve Waite of the key. Don't worry about it. We will get to the ammunition."

Ed Sorenson stood up and stretched. "Okay. Let's say you can do it. How will we get the message around to all the men? Waite's bunch won't let us congregate . . . and they watch us every minute. If we say more than a few words to each other, they interfere. This will take some explaining, coordinating."

"I'll take care of that," Dan said advisedly. "It will be dangerous, but you don't want to go on with this dark-age captivity forever, do you?"

Sorenson shook his bald head. "No, sir," he replied, clearing his throat, "but we don't want our families slaughtered trying to shake free of our captors, either. Some of us figure the mine has to play out in time. When it does, Waite and his bunch will leave."

"What about the slaves in the mine, Ed? How long will they last?"

Sorenson did not answer for a long moment. Slowly his glance met Dan's. "Guess we've been so wrapped up in our own dilemma, we haven't given much thought to them. You're right, Marshal. But how are we going to coordinate it? How will we get the idea to each man?"

"Let me handle that part," Dan said quickly. "All I want to know is, will you join me? I've ascertained that you are a leader in this town. Others will follow if they know you are with the program."

Sorenson drove his right fist into his left palm. "Sure, I'm with you, Marshal. You understand my caution, though, don't you?"

"Of course I do," said Dan, lifting his frame out of the chair. Looking down at the shorter man, he spoke softly. "Every precaution will be taken, Ed. We will surprise them cold. We'll take them without getting any Welcome people hurt."

"That brings up the third problem," Sorenson said heavily.

"Yes?"

"Those in the most danger will be the ones who are held at the Fireside the moment the revolt begins. Their lives won't be worth a wooden nickel. The most difficult thing to plan will be their safety."

"I have not overlooked that fact, Ed. I've done some thinking on it and I'll do some more."

Sorenson managed a smile. "Good. Good."

"How many men over twenty years old in Welcome?"

The bald man looked at the ceiling, then to the floor. "Uh. Let's see . . ." He repeated the movement again. "I'd say about twenty-eight, maybe twenty-nine."

"Could you make me up a list?"

"Sure."

"I can talk with each man without hindrance," Dan said with a furtive grin. "Waite is nervously waiting for me to complete my investigation and be on my way."

"Marshal, is it true that someone slipped a message

out of here with a passenger on the stage? Is that why you're here?"

"Yep."

"God bless 'em," said Sorenson warmly. "Say, that's another thing, Mister Lewis."

"What's that?"

"The stage. It's nigh on to four days late. I'm afraid Kyle Waite—"

"He did."

"Huh?"

"He found out I was coming on the stage Tuesday. He hired some killers to intercept it. They hit us a few miles this side of Durango. Stage went over a cliff."

"Oh, no!" gasped Sorenson. "Charlie and Bob ... are they—"

"Tally was killed, Ed. Lacy's alive. They shot him up pretty bad, but he'll make it."

Dan quickly filled Ed Sorenson in on the details in brief. Then he headed for the door. "I'm going to see as many of the men as I can before dark. I'll be back in the morning for that list. Don't want to miss any. I'll fill you in on the rest of my plan when I come back."

Dan opened the door. Joe Clary and his partner were leaning against the hitching rail across the street in front of the saloon.

Ed Sorenson spoke quietly. "Thanks, Marshal."

The tall man nodded and closed the door.

CHAPTER TWELVE

Mel Curry had spent two days in bed after eating the hot cigar at the hands of Daniel Colt. Taking in food was next to impossible. Swallowing was a painful task. He consumed only liquid, and that had to be at room temperature. Anything hot or cold would stab the scorched and inflamed tissues like a red-hot iron. While he cursed and swore, Mrs. Curry swabbed his throat periodically with lard dipped in coal oil. This checked the swelling and enhanced healing.

Ralph Dunbar, Curry's foreman, sat beside the bed on the afternoon of the second day. He tried to hold his face expressionless while the big man gagged and moaned during a swabbing. As Mrs. Curry left the room, smothered oaths rolled from beneath his rigid mustache. Speaking softly, the boss of the Circle C said, "I'm gonna kill that—"

Mrs. Curry was back in the room, skirts swishing. She was a portly woman who detested profanity. As she busied herself about the room, Curry swallowed hard, watching her movements. Tossing him a stiff glare, she said, "You're going to kill *what?*"

Lowering his head onto the pillow, he said, "That ...*man*. The one who did this to me."

Again she left the room. Mel Curry rolled his bloodshot eyes and fixed them on Dunbar. "I want that blue-eyed bird captured and brought here, Ralph. I mean it."

Dunbar shifted his position nervously. "Boss, that

ain'ta gonna be easy. The boys are gonna be a mite squeamish since you told 'em he was Dan Colt."

Curry swore. Twisting his face in pain, he said, "There's fourteen of you and only one of him."

"I know, boss," Dunbar said, his face flushing, "but that sharpie won't be taken without killin' some of us. None of the boys wants to be the ones whut gits kilt!"

Curry swore again.

"Boss, we remember hearin' stories about this fella Colt. He's faster'n unleashed lightnin' and deadlier'n a mad rattler. A fella over Kansas way told me—"

"I know his reputation," Curry blurted. "I also know I want the pleasure of killing him and dropping his carcass six feet in the sod."

"The boys will be hard to convince, boss. Goin' after Colt is like chasin' a cougar with a slingshot."

Curry swallowed carefully. He rolled his eyes, thinking quietly for an extended moment. Swallowing again, he said, "Best way to hunt a cougar, Ralph, is to make *him* come to *you*. That way, you can fortify yourself and be ready for him."

Dunbar shook his head and blinked his eyes. "You lost me, there, boss."

"Remember what he said just before we left?"

"Yeah. If you bothered the Dolans again, he'd come after you."

"Uh-huh. So we will just work out a little plan to ruffle Dolan's feathers . . . and Colt will come here. We'll set him a trap. Then I'm going to dance on his grave!"

Ralph Dunbar smiled wickedly. "I'll hum the tune for you, boss!"

"I'm getting out of this bed in the morning," Curry said, his face set in stubborn lines. "You come about seven o'clock. I'll have the plan worked out by then."

Morning came with the promise of more snow melting under the warm rays of the Colorado sun. As

Ralph Dunbar stepped onto the porch of the ranch house, a long icicle lost its grip on the eave and plummeted earthward. Mrs. Curry admitted him into the kitchen with a grunt and went about her business. Mel Curry was seated at the breakfast table, sipping lukewarm coffee.

"Mornin', boss," Dunbar said with a smile.

"Sit down," Curry answered, shoving back a chair with his foot.

"You got the plan worked out?"

"Sure do." The big man exposed his teeth in a wide smile.

Dunbar fished the makings out of a shirt pocket and commenced building a cigarette.

"How many head we got this side of the gulch?" Curry asked, setting his cup on the table and pushing it away.

"About five, six hunnerd."

"Good. That oughtta do it."

"Do what?" Dunbar ran his tongue along the thin white paper and pressed it together over the tobacco.

"Fix Dolan so's he'll sell . . . and bring Colt to us."

Dunbar hung the cigarette on his lower lip and thumbed a match into flame. He lifted the match toward his face. "What's the cattle got to do with it?"

"Stampede."

Dunbar's hand froze with the match two inches from the tip. His mouth dropped open, letting the cigarette fall. It touched his lap, rolled to his knee, and fell to the floor. Holding his gaze on Curry's hard eyes, he fished for the cigarette with his fingertips. "Stampede?"

"Yeah. Stampede. We'll just run the herd through Dolan's place and rearrange his furniture. If we aim the bulk at the barn, they'll tear out the corral fence, demolish the sheds, and destroy his equipment.

Maybe we can steer them enough to rip the porch off the house."

Dunbar's fingers had not yet located the cigarette. However, the descending flame on the match in the other hand located his thumb and forefinger. He let out a howl, dropping the match. It fell into a puddle of melted snow from his boots, hissed briefly, and went out.

Curry ejected a belly laugh. Dunbar stuck the burning members in his mouth, then extracted them. Blowing softly on them, he said, "Somebody could get killed, boss."

"Possible. But unlikely," Curry said without feeling.

"What about the law?"

Mel Curry flung his palms upward and hunched his shoulders.

"Can I help it if wolves spook my cattle and they stampede?"

Dunbar wet his fingers and shook them. "Why not set fire to his barn? Either way it'll hurt Dolan, and Colt will know who was behind it."

"One way or another I'm going to get Dolan's place, Ralph. I don't mind throwing up a few sheds and repairing fence, but I don't want to have to build another barn."

"Guess you're right. Anyway, like I said, Colt will know the stampede was no accident. He'll come for you."

A wicked gleam touched Curry's eyes. "Yeah. And we'll be waiting for him. I'm going to bury him right on top of that hill just south of the barn. You know, by that big cottonwood tree."

Dunbar nodded.

"He'll have a nice view from there," Curry said with a laugh.

Dunbar joined in the laughter. "Hey, that's pretty good, boss." He threw back his head and laughed heartily. "*He'll have a nice view from there!* That's really good. From up there he'll be able to see Dolan's place!"

Both men enjoyed Curry's humor for several minutes. Then Ralph Dunbar eased his grin and said, "When's the big stampede, boss?"

"We'll give it another day. Let the snow melt down some. Tell the boys we'll do it tomorrow. We'll make it somewhere's just before noon. After they cut through the Curry place, bring them around to the north. Have a couple of the boys head back and fix our fence. We'll have to let the cattle break it down to look right."

At the same moment Mel Curry and Ralph Dunbar were plotting the stampede, Dan Colt knocked on Nellie Rice's door. The door opened, revealing the lady's freshly powdered face. "Good morning," she said with a smile.

"You want some breakfast?" the tall man asked, twirling his hat on an extended forefinger.

"I could use some coffee," she replied, reaching for her purse, which lay on the dresser. As she closed and locked the door, she looked up at Dan. "Missed you at supper last night. I was worried something might have happen— What happened to your face?"

Dan's fingers found the scab on his cheek. "I'll tell you all about it over ham and eggs." Dan asked about her cold as they descended the stairs and was pleased to know it was better.

As Dan settled Nellie at the table in the hotel dining room, he saw Annie Rankin swing through the kitchen door, carrying a tray of food. She carried it to a table where four hard cases were seated. They were laughing and talking exuberantly. Dan recognized them. These were the new hired guns who had ridden into town the day before. *There would have been five around the table,* Dan thought to himself, *if the man with the hot temper hadn't shot the roan, then thrown his gun on me.*

One of the men eyed Dan as he took his seat opposite Nellie Rice. Turning toward his three cohorts, he jerked his head toward the tall blond man and said something Dan could not distinguish. The others turned and glared at him.

Dan set his eyes on Nellie. "Sorry I missed supper with you last night, but I was busy doing a little visiting around and I got tied up."

"Are things coming together for your plan?" Nellie asked quietly.

Dan was about to answer when Annie Rankin approached the table. Smiling from ear to ear, she said, "What'll it be, Marshal?"

"Mrs. Rice would like coffee."

"Anything else?"

Nellie shook her head. "No, thank you."

"What about you, big boy?"

"Ham, eggs, biscuits, and gravy. Plenty of coffee," Dan answered with a smile that revealed his white, even teeth.

"How do you like your eggs?" Annie asked.

"Oh, I *really* like 'em!" Dan said with a twinkle in his pale blues.

"A comedian, no less," Annie said to Nellie, who was covering her mouth, trying to stifle a burst of laughter. "You oughtta be on the stage, Marshal," she said to Dan. "There's one comes through town every once in a while. They call it Wells Fargo." All three looked at one another and laughed.

"I'll be back with the coffee in a jiffy," said Annie.

As she walked away, Dan said to Nellie, "I bet she could put a hundred-pound sack of flour under each arm and carry them from Missouri to California."

Nellie smiled and shook her head. "Really, Marshal!"

Suddenly one of the hard cases raised his voice and

ejected a string of blue swear words. Another voiced some raw words. All four laughed heartily.

Dan threw a hard glance in their direction just as a third one spewed out a lewd oath. Anger welled through him as Nellie turned the color of fresh strawberries.

Slowly Dan eased back his chair, unbuckled, and stood to full height. He walked to the occupied table. The four men watched his approach. They continued laughing until he spoke.

"In case you boys hadn't noticed," he said through clenched teeth, "you're not in a saloon." Swinging a thumb over his shoulder, he said, "There's a lady present. Now, I would take it kindly if you would curtail the foul language."

Dan had not noticed big Annie's approach. She stood behind him, with one arm behind her back. The one called Wrigley said, "Tell the lady we're sorry, mister."

A younger one dropped his fork hard on the table. "I ain't sorry. Don't you go apologizin' for me, Bert. I can talk any way I want, any old time I want." Dan had commenced to move toward him when Annie quickly stepped around him and brought a heavy skillet down on the young gunman's head. The skillet rang like a church bell. His eyes rolled back in his head, and he fell sideways out of the chair.

The man to his left started to stand up. Annie jumped behind him and, clapping both hands on his shoulders, flopped him back in his chair. He began to curse her. She palmed the back of his neck with her right hand, and sinking the left into his hair, she smashed his face down fiercely. It went straight into his plate of biscuits and gravy.

He tried to work himself free, but the big woman was too strong. She raised his head and slammed his face down repeatedly. Gravy splattered all over the table and speckled the clothing of the other two men.

They sat motionless, indicating that they wanted no part of tangling with big Annie. Dan Colt simply stood by and watched.

When the gunman went limp, Annie relaxed her grip on him. Slowly he slid to the floor.

"I would suggest you two take your friends and get them out of here," Dan said firmly.

Later, when Annie brought breakfast to Nellie Rice and Dan Colt, the latter said, "Annie, remind me to stay on your good side. I don't ever want you mad at me."

Lifting the plates from the tray and placing them on the table, Annie said, "Just don't cuss in front of no ladies in my restaurant, and we'll get along fine." With a big smile and a toss of her head she swaggered back to the kitchen.

"You were going to tell me how the plan is progressing," said Nellie, picking up her cup.

By the time Dan had cleaned his plate, Nellie knew about the layout of the mine and his encounter with the man on the mountainside. She learned that he had talked with nineteen of Welcome's men and that they were ready to back him in his scheme to overcome the outlaws. Some were a little hesitant at first. They feared for the safety of their families. Their hesitancy had faded as Dan explained the procedure. Nellie agreed it was good as he detailed it for her.

As they stood up to leave, Annie approached the table. "Marshal, Ray Henning told me about your plan. If you need my help, let me know. I'm pretty good with a Winchester."

"I bet you are, Annie," said Dan with a broad grin. "Maybe I ought to just turn you loose and let you mop up the whole gang."

Annie Rankin tugged at her left ear. "I might start by whippin' me a U.S. marshal," she said, tilting her head and looking at him out of the tops of her eyes.

As Nellie and Dan reached the top of the staircase

in the hotel, they noticed that the door of room number one was open. As they paused and glanced in, Mrs. Bailey saw them and hurried toward the door.

"He's awake," she said in a half-whisper.

"Oh, good!" gasped Nellie.

Dan eyed the young man lying in the bed. His eyes were open. He was studying the ceiling.

"How long has he been awake?" asked Nellie.

"Just a few minutes," answered Flora Bailey. She looked up at the tall man. "Are you going out right away, Marshal?"

"Soon as I make a quick stop in my room," he replied.

"Will you inform those dirty-looking men down there in the lobby that he is conscious? I'm supposed to let them know right away."

"Sure will," said Dan.

"I'll be back in a few minutes to sit with you, Flora," Nellie said cheerfully.

"Thank you, my dear," said Mrs. Bailey, returning to the bed.

As Dan entered the hotel lobby a few minutes later, he stopped and talked to the desk clerk in hushed tones for several moments. Waite's two guards studied them closely but did not interfere. Getting an affirmative answer, Dan turned and said to himself, *Twenty*.

Crossing to the two men, he said, "Mrs. Bailey asked me to tell you that the boy has regained consciousness." With that he slipped through the door and headed for the Wells Fargo office. He would need Ed Sorenson's list to complete the task.

CHAPTER THIRTEEN

"I told you bird dogs yesterday to stay clear of that U.S. marshal," Kyle Waite said with a scowl. "You get him riled, we'll have real trouble. He's been nosin' around all over town. We'll be rid of him purty soon if we keep things calm."

"Sorry, boss," said Bert Wrigley. "We was mindin' our own business. He come over to our table and started the trouble."

"How did big Annie get in on it?" queried Waite, taking a draw on his cigar.

"Don't know, boss," said Wrigley. "She just come in out of the blue and whanged Smiley on the noggin."

Leo Smiley rubbed his swollen head.

"Then she sunk her claws in Virgil's head and beat his face into his plate."

"I think my nose is broke," added Virgil Sorge, touching it tenderly.

Waite scanned the faces of Bert Wrigley and Don Gregg. "How come you two ain't banged up?"

"I wasn't about to tangle with that big woman! She must rassle grizzly bears for exercise," ejaculated Gregg.

"Me neither," added Wrigley.

"All right, boys," said Kyle Waite, "you get to your posts . . . and stay away from Wilford Lewis. You hear?"

All four acknowledged Waite's commandment and filed out the office door. As they opened the outer door, one of the men stationed at the Mayflower lobby was running in their direction at full speed. It was Lippy Norgren. "What's goin' on?" asked Bert Wrigley as Norgren crowded past them.

"Ain't got time to explain," he said. "Gotta see the boss!"

Kyle Waite answered the rapid knock on his door with an inarticulate grunt. The door opened and the breathless man entered.

"What is it, Lippy?" Waite's husky voice demanded.

"It's Louie Stokes, boss. He's awake!"

"Good!" roared Waite. Rising from his desk chair, he said, "Where's the marshal?"

"I dunno, boss," Norgren answered quickly.

"Did you see him leave the hotel? Or is he still there?"

"He left a little while ago, and I haven't seen him since," said Lippy nervously.

Kyle Waite strapped on his gun, shouldered his massive frame into his coat, and lifted a large Stetson off a wall peg. The smaller man had to almost run in order to keep up with the big man's gait.

The slender desk clerk looked up as Kyle Waite moved through the hotel lobby. The big man bounded up the stairs. Each one creaked under his weight. Lippy remained in the lobby with Alfredo Saldivar.

The door was closed. Waite turned the knob and swung it open. Ignoring the two women who sat beside the bed, he stepped immediately to the boy, whose eyes were closed. "Louie!" he boomed.

The youth did not respond.

"*Louie!*" Waite cursed. "I thought he had come to," he said, looking at Flora Bailey.

"He did," she retorted with a cold look. "But he's out again now."

"Can't you make him wake up again?" Kyle Waite's voice filled the room like angry thunder.

"The boy is in serious condition, Mr. Waite. He will have to come out of it in his own time. To me, it's a wonder that he's alive at all."

"Well, whaddya think?" he said, scowling. "How soon do you think he'll come out of it again?"

"I'm not a doctor," Flora snapped, "but I would say that it is a good sign, his being awake for a few minutes."

"Did he say anything?"

"He asked for Huey. I told him Huey was not here. Then he just stared at the ceiling. I tried to talk to him, but he wouldn't respond. After a few minutes he was out again."

Waite turned his hard glare on Nellie Rice. "Who are you?"

"I'm Nellie Rice," she answered flatly.

"You belong in this town?"

"I live on a ranch south of here, if it's any of your business." There was fire in her eyes. "Do *you* belong in this town?"

Ignoring her, he spoke to the older woman. "You let me know when he is awake enough to talk. I want the description of the man who gunned him down. Got it?"

"Got it," Flora rasped. *Next time I'll wait till he's been awake a good long while,* she told herself.

Waite strode to the door and paused, filling the doorway. "Mrs. Bailey," he said, looking her in the eye, then shifting his gaze to Nellie, then back to Flora.

"Yes," she responded.

"How's your husband?"

Flora Bailey drew her lips in a thin line, turned, and studied Louie Stokes's pallid face. Waite hesitated a few seconds, then turned and descended the stairs.

Tears glistened on Flora's cheeks as she adjusted

the covers on Louie Stokes's shoulders. She felt a hand grip her arm from the other side of the bed.

"Flora," Nellie said softly.

The older woman wiped the tears away with the back of her hand. She sniffed, biting her lip.

"Flora. We've spent hours together. You have never once weakened and told me what was going on here. I know you fear for your husband's life."

Flora's eyes widened. "You *know*?"

Nellie nodded. "Yes. Marshal Lewis has the whole picture and has shared it with me. My husband is laboring in the mine."

Flora Bailey heaved a sigh of relief. "Oh, Nellie, I so much wanted to share it with you, but they're holding Howard—" At this point she broke down and began to sob. Nellie moved quickly and closed the door. Returning to Flora, she embraced her until the sobbing had subsided.

Louie Stokes remained motionless.

Sitting down beside Flora, Nellie said, "Flora, this nightmare will soon be over. The marshal is working on it right now. He is a wise and brave man. I believe in him. He is going to break up this whole thing."

"Oh, I hope so," said Flora, sniffing.

Nellie explained Dan Colt's plan to Flora Bailey. The break would come at sunrise on the next morning. Flora replied that it was too bad blood was going to be shed on the Lord's day. Nellie had lost track of the days. Sure enough, tomorrow would be Sunday. Marshal Lewis had already been assured that nineteen of Welcome's men would fight with him and was optimistic that the rest would join in.

Having spent a little more time with George Keighley, Marshal Lewis had learned that six guards were stationed at the mine. In addition to Keighley and Waite, there were seventeen men positioned about the town. One man guarded the hostages. Two stayed in the Mayflower lobby. Eight men worked twelve hour shifts, watching both ends of the town from abandoned buildings: This put two at each end of town at all times while the other four slept at the Mayflower. There were two at the saloon during business hours. Three others were to mill about during the daytime, watching for any sign of trouble. These same three worked the switching of hostages and were responsible for seeing that the residents were in their homes at night. An hour after sunrise each morning they would take a head count, making sure no one had left town during the night. One other man guarded the gun shop by staying in the abandoned barber shop next door.

Twenty-five in all.

The marshal's plan was to overpower the eighteen men in the town first. George Keighley, protecting his own hide, was now an ally. After subduing the eighteen, they would attack the mine. If all the townsmen cooperated, there would be twenty-nine against eighteen. Flora Bailey was concerned about the hostages. Waite had given orders they were to be shot immediately if trouble developed in the town. Nellie assured her that Marshal Lewis had taken this into account.

Kyle Waite had showed George Keighley where he kept the key for the heavy gun-shop door. It was on the same nail which held a picture on the wall of Waite's office. As far as anyone else knew, Waite carried the key on his person.

Keighley was to obtain the key, then call on the gun-shop guard at midnight. The marshal would wait in the shadows to aid Keighley if needed and to make sure that access had been gained to the ammunition.

Feeling secure that none of the residents would leave the town, Waite had no one watching the houses on the mountainsides. After all, what resident would want to cause the execution of the hostages?

Free to move about at night, except for the extreme ends of the town, the men would make their way to the gun shop at intervals and load their guns.

Outnumbering the outlaws, the townsmen could spread out and be ready for action at Marshal Lewis's signal.

Flora Bailey was elated to know that soon Welcome's trial would be over. Hardly had Nellie finished her explanation when Louie Stokes groaned and rolled his head.

Immediately the older woman turned her attention to the youth. Nellie returned to the other side of the bed.

"Too bad, isn't it?" said Flora.

"What's that?" Nellie asked.

"A young boy like this, an outlaw." Flora shook her head. "Probably led into it by that brother who got killed in the saloon."

Louie opened his eyes. He looked around for a moment, then tried to focus on Flora's face. Rolling his tongue in his mouth, he said weakly, "Where's Huey?"

"He's not here," Flora said softly. "I'm Mrs. Bailey. This is Mrs. Rice," she said, gesturing toward Nellie.

Louie rolled his dark eyes, fixing them on the younger woman. Looking back at Flora, he said, "Huey's dead, isn't he?" His eyes lost their glaze and seemed to focus clearly. Suddenly lifting his head from the pillow, he said, "I remember now. The tall gunslick. He killed Huey."

Flora leaned over him. "Don't excite yourself, son," she said with a touch of authority. "You've been injured seriously."

Louie laid his head back and raised a hand to the thick bandage on his head. "He didn't kill me, did he? He tried, but I'm still alive." Turning to Flora, he said with anticipation, "Are any of the others alive?"

"No, son," she said softly, "they're all dead. You are the only one who lived through it."

Louie seemed to gain strength. Suddenly his face convulsed with a dark, livid hatred. Setting his jaw and lowering his eyelids halfway, he said, "I'm gonna track him down and kill him." Widening his eyes until they bulged, he hissed, "Wait'll he sees me drawin' a bead on him! I won't kill him till he sees my face. Then I'll pull the trigger."

Saliva was running from the corner of his mouth. He laughed heavily. "Yeah. *Then* I'll pull the trigger and send him to Hell with my face burned into his mind. He thought he killed me. Wait'll he sees my f—"

"Louie, you've got to calm down," Flora said hastily. "You're in no condition to let yourself behave this way."

Louie let his head settle on the pillow. He let out a big sigh. "Yeah. That no-good gunslick is gonna be mighty surprised when he sees ole Louie alive and aimin' a gun on him."

He closed his eyes, muttered along the same lines for a minute, then fell asleep.

Flora Bailey knew by Louie's breathing that it was only sleep. He had not slipped back into the coma.

"When he wakes up again, we'll get some broth from Annie Rankin's kitchen for him. He'll get better faster with some food in his innards."

"In one way, that's going to be bad, Flora. He will probably go after that gunfighter as soon as he can walk," Nellie said sadly.

"I'm sure you are right, Nellie. The gunfighter will kill him for sure, next time."

It was just past noon when Dan Colt walked out of the town marshal's office. He closed the door behind him and smiled. George Keighley would have the gun-shop door key by ten o'clock. Kyle Waite had made a habit of playing cards and drinking with two or three men each night. The game was always held in the living quarters behind the Empire Saloon, adjacent to his office. They would begin around eight o'clock and play till after eleven. By ten o'clock they would have plenty of whisky in them and would be talking loudly. George would slip into the office, take the key off the nail, and they would never know it. Within ten minutes the gun-shop guard would be incapacitated, the door unlocked, and the key back on the nail.

Dan angled across the street and headed toward the Wells Fargo office. Ed Sorenson saw him coming and opened the door. Looking across the street, he eyed Joe Clary and his partner sitting on a bench in front of the saloon. Both men were watching him.

"Come in, Marshal," Sorenson said with a straight face.

Dan entered, and the bald man closed the door. "Those two coyotes ever do anything but eyeball you?" Dan asked, looking back through the window.

"Dunno," said Ed. "They're over there most of the time. They paid me another visit about two hours ago."

"Really? What'd they want?" Dan asked, tilting his Stetson to the back of his head.

"They wanted to be sure I hadn't told you anything."

"Did you convince them?"

"I think so. They brought up my wife again." Sorenson mopped his hairless pate. "Marshal, this thing has got to work. I can't stand much more of this. How can men be so cruel?"

"Greed does strange things to a man, Ed," Dan said with a sigh. "My mother showed me in the Bible once where it says that the love of money is the root of all evil. Hit the nail square on the head, wouldn't you say?"

"Can't disagree with that, Marshal," Sorenson answered with a weak smile. "How'd you make out? Everybody ready to fight?"

"To a man," Dan said with a grin. "Everything is set. The showdown is at sunrise. We'll have everybody's gun loaded and their pockets full of shells by twelve thirty. We can all get a good night's sleep."

"I'll sleep better when it's done," Sorenson said, wagging his head.

"The guard with the hostages lets them go to the outhouse one at a time. I hung around the Fireside till I figured out the pattern. He always lets Bailey go last. So I hid and counted till it was Bailey's turn. As soon as the third one reentered the hotel, I made a dash for the outhouse."

Sorenson smiled widely. "And you waited till Howard Bailey entered, then talked to him."

"Correct," Dan grinned. "He knows that at dawn I'm coming to knock on the door. He will alert the other hostages. We want them out of danger before we commence the revolution."

"I knew you'd do it right," Sorenson said with feeling.

"There's an old wagon wheel hanging on a nail behind the outhouse. When the Fireside guard is out of commission, I'll roll that wagon wheel across the street. That's the signal. When it appears, everybody goes into action."

"Sounds good, Lewis," Sorenson said.

"The minute the sun gives us enough light, so we don't shoot each other, I'll roll it."

"You ever been in the army?" Sorenson asked.

"Nope."

"You should have been," Sorenson said, placing a hand on Colt's broad shoulder. "You'd have made a good general!"

"Let's talk about it when the thing is over," Dan

said with a slight blush. "We'll see how you feel about me then."

Dan strode to the door.

"See you at midnight, Marshal."

Dan nodded. "Midnight." The door closed behind him. He ignored Clary and his cohort as he headed up the street for the livery stable. *Might as well confuse their thinking,* he said to himself.

Within a few minutes inquisitive eyes of both friend and foe watched him trot the bay out of town. This time he headed north.

The trees were shedding snow in a hurry now. The sun felt warm on his back. He rode for over an hour, thinking through his whole plan of attack, trying to weed out any flaws. He could find none. If each man did his job, Welcome would be free by eight o'clock tomorrow morning.

Dan topped a high ridge and looked down into a vast and beautiful valley. Off in the distance he could see Ouray. The town looked like a series of little toy buildings as it lay quietly in the Colorado sun.

As he headed back for Welcome, he thought of Lily Dolan. "One more lonely, agonizing night, Lily," he said audibly, "and you will have your husband back."

Dan thought what a lucky man Tom Dolan was to have a woman like Lily to go home to. His mind flashed back to his Wyoming ranch. Mary. Beautiful, sweet, loving Mary. Why was she taken from him? He never had deserved her. But she loved him. They had so much together. Why did it have to end so suddenly? So brutally?

Dan shook his head. No sense in feeling sorry for himself. Nothing could change what had happened. He just had to get this Welcome mess straightened out. Then he could resume pursuit of his outlaw twin. Someday he would capture Dave and clear himself with the law. And then . . . then . . . Dan shrugged his shoulders. You can't cross a bridge until it lays at your feet.

The sun was lowering against the western mountains as Dan rode back into Welcome. His gaze fell on the high peaks to the southeast, toward the mine. He wondered if anyone had found the dead man on the mountain.

Dismounting at the livery stable, he handed the reins to the hostler.

"Is everything all set, Marshal?" the hostler asked.

"All set," Dan said with a note of assurance.

As he passed Lippy Norgren and Alfredo Saldivar in the Mayflower lobby, he adjusted his gunbelt. Pausing at the desk, he spoke in a voice inaudible to Waite's henchmen. "Bullets at midnight."

The clerk dipped his chin in acknowledgment.

As Dan topped the stairs, he stepped in through the open doorway of Louie Stokes's room. The youth was propped up against several pillows, holding a bowl of broth in one hand and wielding a spoon with the other.

"Good evening, Marshal," said Flora Bailey.

"Hello," Nellie chirped.

"Looks like you ladies have been good medicine for your patient. I see he's up and taking nourishment."

Louie's ears caught the voice. Nellie saw him look up at Dan's face. There was clearly recognition in his eyes. His face blanched. The bowl slipped from his fingers, spilling broth on the blankets. Both women jumped to their feet. Nellie retrieved the bowl as Flora Bailey ran to the washstand for a towel.

Sensing the electricity in the air and considering the look on Louie's face, Nellie moved swiftly to the door. "We've got to clean up this mess, Marshal. Knock on my door in half an hour, and I'll walk you to supper."

"All right," he said, touching the brim of his hat. "The boy seems to be pretty edgy."

"Yes, he's quite nervous," she answered, swinging the door. "See you shortly."

"Yes, ma'am," said Dan, moving down the hall. As the door clicked shut, he wagged his head. "The boy looked at me like he'd seen a ghost," he chuckled.

Inside the room Louie Stokes wiped a trembling hand over his face. Looking at Flora, he said, "You know you said I could see Mr. Waite a little later?"

"Yes, Louie."

"I want to see him *right now!*"

CHAPTER FOURTEEN

"I've been thinkin', Miss Lily," said Charlie Lacy, "Dan's been gone nearly three days now . . ."

Lily Dolan was leaning moodily against the kitchen door, looking through the window. Her gaze was fixed on the road as it wound its way northward toward Welcome. Slowly she turned, letting her dull eyes meet those of the rawboned shotgunner, who sat at the table.

"I'll be ready to ride by Monday. Instead of me headin' fer Durango, why don't we just take the buckboard and you 'n' me 'n' the kids'll head for Welcome?"

The total despair written on Lily Dolan's face was worrying Lacy. His strength was slower returning than he had anticipated. He had hoped to recover sufficiently to ride to Durango by now. As Saturday had dawned, he found that his head still grew light when he stood up, and there was yet much pain in the wounded shoulder when he moved.

During the day he had forced himself to walk around the room. The dizziness had subsided some, but even by late afternoon he knew it would take at least two more days to gain sufficient strength for the trip.

Lily brushed back a wisp of hair which dangled defiantly on her forehead. "You told Dan you would ride to Durango and send him help," she said listlessly. "If they are still alive, whoever or whatever is holding them would be too much for us to handle."

Lacy took a sip of steaming coffee. "But, Miss Lily," he whined, "it looks to me that not knowin' what's happenin' at Welcome is takin' its toll on you. I can't let you suffer like this."

"I'll be all right, Charlie," replied Lily, forcing a smile. "The main thing is to get help to Dan." The stubborn wisp was on her forehead again.

A playful squeal was heard from the bedroom, followed by a series of giggles.

Lily smiled again. "Oh, for the sweet innocence of childhood."

The old man grinned and shook his head. "Yep," he cackled, "a wise old Indian I used to know always said that youth was wasted on the young."

Lily crossed to the stove and moved the hissing coffeepot from over the fire. "Let's proceed as planned," she said. "You ride to Durango Monday. If the men are still alive, they are in trouble. The best thing for them is to send in men who can help them. It would do no good for us to fall into the same situation."

"I jist hate to see a purty thing like you hurtin' inside," Lacy said tenderly.

"Bless your sweet heart, Charlie, I appreciate your concern, but we must do what's best for Tom, Bill, and Dan." She brushed the wisp back again. "I think I will ride over and check on Nellie Rice in the morning, if you will watch the children."

Lacy's brow furrowed. "I don't know, Miss Lily," he said heavily, "that might be dangerous with that there Mel Curry around. From what you tell me, he's a bad 'un. Mebbe you hadn't ought to go meanderin' off by yourself."

"I'll be just fine, *grandma*," she said, patting his shoulder. "After the whipping Dan gave him, I'm sure he won't be bothering me again." The obstinate wisp was down again.

"It could work just the opposite, ma'am," said Charlie, squaring his jaw. "Curry jist might be chuck full of vengeance by now. He could git real mean. Whyn't you jist stay right here, where you're reasonably safe?"

"Nellie has got to be worried sick, just like I am. Maybe we can help each other. I'm really not afraid."

Lacy flopped a palm on the table. "I declare, you are jist as stubborn as that lock of hair that keeps fallin' on your forehead!"

Lifting her eyes upward to look at the coal-black wisp, Lily extended her lower lip and blew hard. It lifted and landed in the same place. She looked straight into the shotgunner's eyes, attempting a trace of humor.

A tight grin tugged at the corners of Lacy's mouth. A twinkle touched his eye as he said, "You ain't too big to be spanked, young lady. I might jist take a notion to turn you over my knee and whop you good!"

Lily laughed. "You old scalawag. You might say things to make me laugh and forget my troubles, but you wouldn't spank me, now, would you?"

The prevailing tension eased as Lacy grinned sheepishly and broke into a laugh, joining with hers. After a moment things were quiet as Lily turned to the cupboard to begin supper preparations. The Wells Fargo shotgunner studied the back of her head several minutes. Then he spoke.

"Miss Lily."

"Mm-hmm."

"I *will* whop you, though, if . . ."

Looking over her shoulder, she said, "If what?"

"If you ever call me *grandma* again!"

They laughed together once more as darkness fell over the land.

Dan Colt closed the door and locked it behind him. He tossed his hat on a chair and stretched out on the bed. He had a half hour to wait before going to supper with Nellie Rice. Lacing his fingers together, he cupped his hands behind his head.

As he thought over his well laid plan to set Welcome free, he was satisfied that if it was executed properly, little blood would be shed. The townsmen would all take their positions so as to have the drop on every one of the outlaws. They would have the element of surprise, and they were greater in number.

Dan was sure there would be one or two foolhardy outlaws who would try to shoot their way out. Someone, no doubt, was going to get killed. Over all, though, he felt easy. At the moment he would give the signal, most of the outlaws would just be rousing from slumber. What few were out of bed would be groping about sleepy-eyed, their minds still foggy.

The guards at each end of the town would be the hardest to take alive. Dan was doubling his forces there, to ensure success.

As he thought over the carefully planned strategy, something kept picking at his mind. For a moment he thought of the strange look in Louie Stokes's eyes. There was fear in them. Like he had seen a ghost. But there was more than fear. There was a kind of recognition. Louie seemed to know him.

Dan shrugged off the thought. *How could Louie—* There were heavy footsteps at the end of the hall. They had sounded on the steps and halted at the top. A door opened. A heavy voice spoke sharply. Dan thought he detected Flora Bailey's voice. The door slammed shut.

Someone had entered Louie's room and ejected Mrs. Bailey. Dan could hear her talking as she descended the stairs to the lobby.

An uneasiness crept over him. Rolling off the bed, he fumbled momentarily in the gathering darkness and struck a match. After lighting the lantern, he produced the pocket watch from his vest. It was time to knock on Nellie's door.

Dan Colt had courted danger and brushed close to death most of his adult life. A man who lives by the gun develops an indescribable instinct. A little bell rings somewhere back in the chambers of his mind. He does not hear it with his ears but with the raw ends of his nerves.

The little bell was ringing clearly.

From the top of the dresser, next to the lantern, Dan lifted a match. Carefully he bent it until it snapped, making sure it did not break in two. Forming it into a perfect L, he unlocked and opened the door. Swinging the door until it was ajar only by inches, he reached up and placed the broken match at the top of the door to the hinge side. Hanging the match over the edge by the short end, he pulled the door shut. The long end was barely visible. A person would have to be looking for it to see it. Locking the door and pocketing the key, he crossed the narrow hall and tapped on Nellie's door.

"Your escort has arrived, madam," said Dan Colt as Nellie opened the door.

A faint smile rode her lips as she stepped into the hallway. Dan could see that the smile did not reach her eyes. She was troubled but was desperately trying to hide it. Turning the key in the lock, she placed her hand in the crook of the tall man's arm.

Together they moved down the hall toward the stairs. As they passed Louie Stoke's room, they could make out his voice. He sounded excited. The deep, heavy voice which Dan had heard earlier was speaking calmly in return.

Nellie looked up at Dan as they reached the stairs. "That's Kyle Waite's voice," she whispered.

"Sounds like the voice of a big man," Dan said idly.

"He is," she assured him. "He's at least two inches taller than you. He probably weighs in the neighborhood of two hundred and seventy pounds. He could probably seesaw with a bull elephant."

Dan chuckled as they reached the lobby floor. "Sounds like some dude."

"That he is," Nellie said flatly. "Tall, dark, and gruesome."

As they settled at their usual table, Dan said, "Mr. Waite sounds like one *hombre* I would not like to tangle with."

Annie Rankin angled toward their table. Dan winked at Nellie and said with a furtive grin, "I'll bet she could whip him!"

As they ate the meal, Dan studied Nellie closely. "You're upset, Nellie. Want to talk about it?"

"It's that boy, Dan," she replied apprehensively.

"That's the first time you've addressed me as *me*," he said, smiling.

Nellie nodded. "I've kept it on the Marshal Wilford Lewis basis so I wouldn't slip inadvertently."

"Uh-huh. I appreciate that." Dan took a mouthful of coffee, swallowed it and said, "Now, what's bothering you? What about the boy?"

"Did you see the look in his eyes when he heard your voice and saw your face?"

"My voice?" Dan asked with surprise.

"Yes. When you appeared at the door, he was looking at his broth. He looked up when he heard you speak as if he knew your voice. It was when he saw your face that he dropped the bowl."

"He thought he knew me. That's for sure," Dan said, nodding.

"Dan, is it possible?"

"I guess it's possible, but I never saw him before as far as I know."

"As soon as you were gone, he asked to see Kyle Waite." Nellie shook her head. "I don't like it, Dan. I have an uneasy feeling in the pit of my stomach. If something goes wrong now, we'll never—"

"Now, Nellie, don't come apart on me. We're going to break this gang and free your husband." Standing up, Dan said, "You're tired. A good night's sleep will make you feel better."

"I hope so," Nellie replied without conviction.

"By this time tomorrow night, you and Bill will be home in your own house, safe and sound," he said reassuringly.

As they passed the desk, Dan eyed the slender clerk. The man's hollow face was ashen gray. There was a pleading in his eyes. Dan wanted to stop, but Waite's night sentinels were standing too close. They would be able to hear any words exchanged.

The tall man ushered Nellie Rice up the stairs.

Louie Stokes's face was drawn tight in harsh lines of bitterness as Kyle Waite's hulking figure entered the door.

"You can take a walk, Mrs. Bailey," Waite said, holding the door.

Flora Bailey drew the shawl about her shoulders and, like a frightened kitten, lowered her head and passed through the doorway.

"Mrs. Bailey . . ." Waite said, scowling down at her.

Fear was evident in her eyes as she met his glare. "Yes."

"Don't go too far." His voice was sharp.

She nodded and headed toward the stairs. Descending them, she spoke to the desk clerk. "That man could use a few manners."

Closing the door hard, as was his custom, Waite approached the bed. "Glad to see you're doing better, Louie. You wanted to see me?"

"You bet I do!" the youth said with emotion. "You know that tall blond *hombre* with the star on his chest?"

Kyle Waite towered over the bed. The flame from

the lantern cast an eerie shadow on his swarthy face. "You mean the U.S. marshal?"

Louie's eyes were bulging with hatred. "He ain't no marshal," Louie said heatedly. *"He's the gunslick who killed Huey and the others and shot me!"*

Waite's bearded jaw loosened. He bent low over Louie Stokes. "Are you sure?"

The youth was having trouble controlling himself. His voice took on a high pitch. "Yes! I'd swear it on my mother's grave! He's the one. No question."

Kyle Waite straightened up and rubbed his whiskers. "Why would he come back here?"

"That's not hard to figure," Louie retorted excitedly. "Huey was gonna put him to work in the mine. He told him the whole operation."

Waite cursed.

"Huey didn't figure it'd hurt, Mr. Waite. He was gonna work him to death in the mine anyhow."

Waite paced back and forth, cursing. "Have I ever been stupid," he growled, wagging his head. "He's been all over this town asking questions. I let him because I thought he was U.S. government. I knew the people wouldn't tell him anything. Figured I'd be rid of him shortly."

"People didn't need to tell him anything," said Louie. "He already knows it."

Kyle Waite cursed again. "He's figurin' out a way to take over the operation, sure as shootin'." The big man slammed a meaty fist into an open palm. His teeth clenched and showed white in contrast to his black beard. "I'm gonna kill him with my bare hands!"

Louie's face twisted. "Oh, no you don't. He killed my brother. I'm the one who's gonna kill him! I'm gonna blow him full of holes."

The youth's voice lifted to a high pitch once more. "Dirty skunk stood right there in that door and acted like he didn't know me." Breathing heavily he hissed, "He'll know me just before I pull the trigger."

Neither man heard the footsteps moving past the door in the hallway.

"Sorry, kid," said Waite. "I'm gonna do the killin' on this bird." His eyes were red with passion. "I'm gonna tear off both his arms and beat him to death with 'em!"

Louie Stokes argued adamantly, but the big man ignored him.

Waite walked to the door and rested his giant hand on the knob. Looking back, he asked, "You keep quiet about this, kid. Did you let on to Mrs. Bailey?"

A sullen shadow had settled on Louie's face. "No. She probably figured out that I recognized him, but that's all."

Waite nodded and opened the door.

"You ain't bein' fair," Louie said evenly. "It was *my* brother he killed. It was *my* head he tried to blow off."

"Tell you what, kid," Waite said huskily, "I'll rip off his head and deliver it to you on a silver platter."

Louie's lower lip formed in a pout as the door slammed shut.

CHAPTER FIFTEEN

The little bell was ringing in the back of Dan Colt's mind with intensity as he escorted Nellie Rice down the hallway. All was quiet in Louie Stokes's room. A soft yellow light shimmered through the crack under the door.

As they approached her room, Dan squeezed Nellie's arm. She looked up at him in the light of the lantern on the wall. He extended his forefinger vertically against pursed lips. Easing noiselessly across the hall, he eyed the broken matchstick lying on the floor. This meant one thing. Someone had entered his room. Perhaps they were still in there.

Turning silently toward Nellie, he motioned for her to step back toward the stairs. Quietly she obeyed, edging her way along the wall.

Dan drew his right-hand Colt and thumbed back the hammer. He lifted his right foot and kicked the door hard. At the same instant he leaped to the side and flattened himself against the wall. The door flew open and banged against the inside wall.

"All right, you can come out now," Dan barked. His voice was sardonic.

He had left his lantern burning. Its soft glow spilled into the hallway.

He heard a slight shuffle come from the room. Then another. A shadow flicked across the open door. In one swift motion he ducked low and swung into the doorway, gun ready. The intruder slipped behind a wardrobe, which extended a couple of feet from the wall.

"Come out right now, mister, or I'll shoot right through it," Dan rasped. "Throw your gun out first."

Immediately a .44 revolver scooted across the floor and went under the bed.

"There it is. Don't shoot!" The owner of the frightened voice appeared, hands raised. Dan recognized one of the hard cases who had used the foul language in the restaurant. It was the man whom Annie Rankin had crowned with the skillet.

"Aren't you in the wrong room?" the tall man snapped.

Leo Smiley managed an artificial smile. "Yeah. I—I guess I musta got in here by mistake."

Dan Colt was hunched forward, framed in the doorway. "It was a mistake, all right," he replied coldly. "Now, just what—"

From down the hall he heard Nellie scream, "Dan! Look out!"

He turned just in time to see a figure emerge through the door of Nellie's room. A large dark object was in his hand. It was coming in a wide arc, aimed for his head.

Dan ducked, and the club thudded into the door jamb. Anger whipped through him like a fanned flame. Before the man could regain his balance, Dan hit him with a sledge-hammer blow, square on the jaw. As he went down, Dan saw that it was Virgil Sorge.

Behind him Smiley was on his belly next to the bed, trying to locate his gun. Dan palmed both .45s, pointing one at Smiley and aiming the other in Sorge's direction. In the hallway Virgil Sorge was scrambling to his feet, shaking his head.

"Both of you hold it right there!" Dan barked.

Smiley eyed the yawning muzzle of the Colt .45 and rolled over slowly, exposing empty hands.

"On your feet," Dan snapped. Looking through the

door at Sorge, he said, "Unbuckle your gunbelt, mister. Slow like."

Sorge started to comply when the sound of heavy footsteps on the stairs reverberated down the hallway. Nellie released a scream, but it was immediately muffled. A slow, malignant smile crept over Sorge's mouth.

Dan did not have to see down the hallway to know what was happening. Someone had seized Nellie Rice and he would be forced into submission to ensure her safety.

"Tell him to give it up, Virgil. I've got his lady friend." The voice from the hallway was cold and calculated.

Virgil Sorge fixed his gaze on Dan Colt. With a note of triumph in his voice he said, "Drop 'em, cowboy, or the lady's funeral will be tomorrow."

Dan could hear Nellie struggling. The assailant had apparently clamped a hand over her mouth. She was emitting a low nasal whine. There was nothing he could do. A parley concerning the two men he held at gunpoint would be useless. The man who held Nellie's life in his hands would know that Dan could not gamble it.

Reluctantly he lowered the twin Colts and let them drop to the floor. Leo Smiley pounced on them. Jumping to his feet, he leveled the muzzles on the tall blond man. "All right, Tate!" Smiley exclaimed. "I got him!"

Virgil Sorge retrieved his club. The twisted smile had not left his lips.

"Bring him out," said Tate Landry.

"Git," Smiley said stiffly.

Dan stepped into the hall. Landry released Nellie, who sagged against the wall. "Go to your room, lady," he said sharply as he pointed his gun at Dan.

Nellie looked at Dan. Fear filled her eyes. There was a pinched white ring around her mouth. He wanted to comfort her. Anything he said now would be empty and in vain. Slowly she slid along the wall and entered the dark room, closing the door.

"Let's go, *Marshal*," Landry said in a mocking tone.

As they reached the stairs, Dan saw George Keighley enter the outside door of the lobby. Lippy Norgren was on his heels. Keighley watched them descend the stairs. There was a look on Keighley's face which Dan Colt had never seen on the face of a man. It was an admixture of surprise, awe, and shock.

"The boss said to take him to the jail and lock him up," Norgren told Landry. "He sent me to get George. Mr. Waite will be down to the jail in a few minutes."

"He's all yours, George," Landry said, holstering his gun.

Keighley quickly drew his own, leveling it at Dan Colt's midsection.

"Let me just crack him a good one," Virgil Sorge said, waving the club with one hand and rubbing his jaw with the other.

"Better not," ejaculated Lippy Norgren. "Mr. Waite said to lock him up and keep him safe. He wants to deal with this imposter personally."

Sorge withdrew, shaking his head. "Just one good wallop wouldn't hurt nuthin'," he said, his voice trailing off.

"Hold it right there!" a high-pitched voice came from the balcony at the top of the stairs. Every eye flitted upward. Louie Stokes was standing at the rail, leaning heavily with both hands. "George, don't you let Waite kill him. He's mine!" Louie's face was livid with fury.

The puzzle was in its last stage of forming into a clear picture for Dan Colt. Louie Stokes would now fit the last piece into place.

"He killed my brother! It was him who left four

men dead over at the saloon and tried to blow my head off! I got a right to kill him!"

It was all in place now. Dan heard Tate Landry order the irate youth back to bed as he thought of four men gunned down and a fifth left for dead. *Dave!*

Dan had been trailing his identical twin through these mountains. There was no question he had come through Welcome. Waite's henchmen had no doubt attempted to seize him for labor in the mine. Dave, like Dan, was fast and deadly with a pair of guns. He had shot his way out and escaped. Louie Stokes was the only living member of Kyle Waite's gang who had seen Dave's face.

Dan rued the moment he had appeared at Louie's door. His masquerade as Wilford Lewis was over. No one here was going to believe he was not the gunman who killed Waite's men at the Rockaway Saloon. They would no more accept the twin brother story than had Marshal Logan Tanner. The latter had arrested him for a crime committed by Dave Sundeen. Dan had gone to Yuma Territorial Prison as *Dave Sundeen.*

"Let's go, mister," said George Keighley, waving his gun toward the door. Dan stepped out into the night. Keighley followed, gun in hand. Leo Smiley walked beside Keighley, carrying Dan's guns.

When they entered the marshal's office, Keighley told Smiley to lay the twin Colts on the desk. He commanded Dan to remove his gunbelt. When Dan had complied, Keighley directed Smiley to holster the Colts and place the gear in a certain desk drawer. This accomplished, he dismissed Smiley and herded Dan through the back door of the office. Moving into the cell area, he locked the tall man in a cell and returned to the office.

A gray mask of vindictive hatred captured George Keighley's face. He went directly to the stove and stirred the fire, carefully placing the poker so the tip would heat up rapidly.

He paced the floor for several minutes, rubbing his hands together. He lifted the poker, examined the tip, and replaced it in the fire. Then he walked back and stood in front of Dan's cell. In the dim light Dan could see that Keighley was bent on no good.

Keighley drew his gun and pointed it at Dan, who sat on the bunk. "Get up and come over here," he said icily. Dan did not move. The thick-bodied man was breathing heavily. His eyes were red with anger. *"I said come over here!"* He thumbed back the hammer.

Dan Colt did not move. "If you shoot me, you'll have Kyle Waite to deal with," he said coolly. "Didn't you hear what Norgren said?"

George Keighley swore vehemently. "I'll tell him you tried to escape, and I had to plug you. Wouldn't be hard to unlock the door and make it look that way after you're dead."

Dan knew Keighley was right. The wrath welling up inside him made him plenty dangerous at this moment. Keighley's eyes widened as Colt slowly rose from the cot and approached the bars.

"So you were gonna help me with the law if I aided in overthrowing Waite, were you, *Marshal?*"

Dan ran his tongue over his white, even teeth. "The people in this town need to be rid of Waite." His ice-blue eyes were fixed hard on the heavy-set man.

"Who are you, mister?"

"You wouldn't believe me if I told you."

Keighley narrowed his eyes and ran his free hand over his upper lip. "Get down on your knees."

Dan eased down to his knees, face to the bars. Keighley reached into a corner and grasped a wooden chair. Turning the chair with the front toward the bars, he shoved it against the cell door. Carelessly wagging the muzzle of the gun, he said,. "Put your hands through the bars. All the way. I want your face against the bars."

Dan knew what was coming. George Keighley was going to put the hot poker to his face. Vengeance was eating him up.

Keighley lifted the chair so Dan's arms would extend around the legs. He handcuffed him in that position. Dan's face was pressed against the bars. Keighley had him where he wanted him. He disappeared momentarily, then reappeared with the smoldering poker in his hand. Sweat beaded on Dan's brow.

"Now we'll see who's gonna kiss the poker, *Marshal*," he said cynically.

"You're overlooking one thing," Dan said hastily.

"Oh?" Keighley smiled. "What's that?"

"If I tell Waite you were going to get us into the gun shop, he'll hang you from the nearest tree."

"It's my word against yours."

"Not quite," Dan said, looking him straight in the eye. "How many men in this town know where Waite keeps the keys to the gun shop?"

"Two," Keighley snapped. "Waite and myself."

"Huh-uh," said Dan. "Three."

Keighley's face blanched.

"If I tell Waite where he keeps the key, he'll know who told me."

Now the sweat was on Keighley's face. "Then I'll just blow your brains out right now and tell him you were trying to escape."

Dan shook the chair. "From this position?"

Keighley changed hands with the poker and wiped sweat from his face.

"He'll be here any minute, Keighley. You sure you've got time to kill me and get everything arranged proper? Somebody will hear the shot. How are you going to explain why it took you so long to lock me up?"

Keighley spun on his heels and disappeared again. Dan heaved a sigh of relief. The heavy-set man returned, minus the poker, and unlocked the handcuffs. He muttered something Dan could not understand as he tossed the chair to its original corner. The starch had left him.

"Listen, George," said Dan, getting to his feet, "one way or another, we're going to break Waite. This town is going to be freed. I'll see to it you ride away, if you'll stick with us."

"Can't happen," said Keighley, shaking his head. "Waite's gonna kill you. I've seen him do it before. He'll beat you to death with his bare fists. I watched him do it to three men. I know of several others."

"Do you mean he gives the other man a sporting chance?"

"Sure. If you can call it that. He'll rule out all weapons. Has to be bare knuckles. Even if he got into trouble, no man would dare interfere. Matter of pride. Waite wants to handle it all by himself." Keighley cocked his head sideways. "You've never seen him, have you?"

"Nope."

"He's big. Mighty big. Couple inches taller than you. Outweighs you fifty, sixty pounds. Strong as a bull ox. Mean. *Bad* mean. He'll try to maim you before he kills you. Saw him once break both arms on a man, then, when he had him helpless, get him on the ground and keep beating him till he was dead."

"George," said Dan thoughtfully, "you've got enough sense to realize that one of these days, even if Waite kills me, this operation is going to come to an end."

"Sure," retorted Keighley, "the mine is bound to play out eventually."

"That's not what I mean. Before that happens, somehow somebody is going to bring the law down on this situation. When they do, if you escape the gallows, George, you'll rot in prison."

Keighley rubbed the back of his neck. "So?"

"If you help me, you'll be doing the people of Welcome a big favor, and you'll be the cause of those slaves in the mine being set free."

George Keighley rubbed his neck some more and studied Dan's face. "How can I help you?"

"Let me out of here. Give me back my guns. Make like I got the jump on you and got away. Give me a few minutes to head for the Empire. I'll wait in back until you start screaming your head off. That'll draw Waite out of his quarters. Tell them I knocked you out, and you just woke up. I'll get the key and head for the gun shop. Then you—"

The front door in the outer office came open loudly. Heavy steps shook the floor as Kyle Waite appeared in the inner doorway. Dan noticed immediately how the giant of a man literally filled it. Slowly the big man approached the cell. George Keighley moved slightly to the side, Waite towering over him. Waite sized Dan Colt up with a wicked eye. His heavy voice filled the room. "So this is our Marshal Wilford Lewis?"

Tate Landry entered slowly behind Waite and stood spread-legged, folding his arms. Dan fixed his pale-blue eyes on the hulking figure of Kyle Waite.

"What *is* your name?" the giant boomed.

"What difference does it make?" Dan rasped coldly.

"I asked you a question, sonny," Waite roared.

"And I asked you one, daddy," Dan retorted, not blinking or disturbing a facial muscle. He had dealt with bullies before. Showing fear is the worst thing to do.

Waite's dark face flushed. "Smart mouth, eh? I'd pull you outta there and tear you apart right now, except it'll be more fun tomorra."

The big man scratched his heavy beard. Dan noticed his nose was scarred and twisted slightly off center. It had been damaged severely at some time and probably broken.

"So you was gonna muscle your way in here and take over, huh? You should have stuck to your gunslingin', sonny. You must be pretty good. Took out four of my best men in one swipe."

Dan thought of how many times he had been blamed for things his outlaw twin had done.

"Tell you what, sonny. You get yourself a good night's rest. George here will bring you a good breakfast at seven. We'll let it settle some, then at nine o'clock we're going to have Sunday school. Tomorra is Sunday, you know."

Waite hunched his massive shoulders, then dropped them. "I'm gonna give you a Sunday school lesson, sonny. One you'll remember all the way to Hell."

Dan's cold stare never flinched. He was wise enough to hold a fearsome respect for a man Waite's size, but Waite would not be made aware of it.

"You do it, then talk about it," Dan said bluntly.

A cynical sneer washed over Waite's dark face. "I will, sonny. I will." He turned and shouldered his way through the door, followed by Keighley and Landry.

Dan's hopes for persuading George Keighley to stage an "escape" were dashed when he heard Kyle Waite say, "Tate, you stay here tonight and help George guard the place. That blond-headed bird is slicker'n axle grease. I want him out there in the street for Sunday school in the mornin'. No slip-ups. You understand?"

"Got it," Dan heard Tate Landry reply. The door banged shut, and Waite was gone.

Dan sat down on the bunk. He could hear Keighley and Landry talking in the outer office. They were speaking in low tones, and he could not make out what they were saying.

He thought about the situation. If somehow Keighley could get the key to the gun shop, the townsmen could go ahead with the uprising. A shaded feeling settled over him. They would not do it without him. He had spearheaded the plan. If he was not there to lead them, they would lack the impetus to carry it through.

Dan wondered if word of his being locked up had spread sufficiently to the townspeople. If not, some of the men would rendezvous at the gun shop, assuming things were on schedule. The guard in the barber shop would probably start shooting. Dan had to be sure every man was alerted. Somehow he must get George Keighley to see that it was done.

The two men were still carrying on their conversation in the outer office. Dan was about to call out to Keighley, hoping he would respond alone, so he could talk to him. Before he could do it, the heavy murmur of voices ceased, and Keighley appeared, followed by Landry. The latter drew close to the cell door.

"Were you crawlin' around the mountain over by the mine yesterday?" he asked, fixing his eyes on Colt.

Dan eyed him as he would a pesky fly or a nagging mosquito. "You writing a book?" the blond man asked in a low monotone.

Landry's lean face grew hard. "Don't smart-mouth me, mister gunfighter," he said in a thick voice. "I might just yank you outta there and give you a little lesson before you get your big one in the morning."

"You and I both know better than that, Landry." Dan stood up and approached the bars. Landry dropped his hand to the butt of his gun. "You're safe," chided the tall man. "I can't get through the bars."

Landry's face was rigid. "We found one of the mine guards dead. Did you kill him?"

"Nope," Dan snapped.

"You were seen riding out of town. You were gone long enough to ride over there and—"

"I didn't say I wasn't over at the mine," Dan said huskily. "You asked if I killed him. I didn't."

"Did you tangle with him?"

"Yep. He threw a gun on me and gave me this," Dan said, pointing to the scab on his cheek.

"You killed him, then," Landry said, eyes widening.

"Nope. We were rolling in the snow. I gave him some bruises, but I didn't kill him. He went to gasping for breath, turned purple, and quit breathing. It was along about there that he died." Dan held his face stiff.

George Keighley, standing behind Landry, caught the dart of Dan's humor and was trying to stifle a laugh. Landry turned around, and Keighley's heavy smile vanished instantly.

"Got any coffee around this place, George?" Landry snapped.

"Yeah," answered Keighley, turning toward the office door. "I'll fix us some."

"Nothin' doin'," said Landry. "I've had your coffee before. I'll fix it." With that he strode through the door, leaving Keighley behind.

CHAPTER SIXTEEN

Sunday morning came with the gray dawn giving way to a flourish of flaming orange, followed by a yellow sun lifting into a cloudless blue sky. Vagrant breezes swayed the branches of the towering evergreens, tugging at the leafless aspens.

Lily Dolan felt the fresh air on her face as she stepped out on the back porch, tossed a pan of soapy water on the ground, and hung the pan on a nail. The air was sweet in her lungs as she breathed deeply, fixing her gaze on the road. As she pointed her freshly washed face northward, she wondered if she would ever see Tom Dolan alive again. Or Bill Rice. Or Dan Colt.

After she had fed the children and Charlie Lacy their breakfast, she would ride over to the Rice ranch and check on Nellie. *Strange, really,* she thought, *that Nellie hasn't come over here before now.*

Standing on the porch for a moment, Lily watched the sunlight dance on the ripples of the gurgling stream. The melting snow had swollen it somewhat.

Suddenly her eyes caught a slight movement against the trees where the road wound toward the south. Riders. Two of them. Lily's throat tightened. Were they Mel Curry's men? They had angled off the road and were headed toward the bridge. Curry's men would not ordinarily come from that direction, but Lily Dolan would take no chances.

Whirling, she darted through the door and

slammed it behind her. Sliding the heavy bolt into its place, she shouted, "Charlie!"

Charlie Lacy was awake but had not bothered to force his aging body off of the couch. He sat up and looked toward the excited woman. "What is it, ma'am?" he asked, fingering the sleep from his eyes.

"Riders coming! Two of them." Lily hoisted the heavy Sharps from its place in the corner and checked the load. As soon as she turned her back to look out the window, the Wells Fargo shotgunner threw the covers back and pulled on his pants. Favoring the arm on the side where he had received the wound, he made his way to the stack of guns confiscated from Mel Curry and his men. He took up a Winchester .44 and levered in a shell. Stepping behind Lily, he peered over her shoulder, squinting his eyes, attempting to bring the approaching riders into focus. They were just crossing the bridge.

Patty Ruth came in from the bedroom, nightgown brushing the tops of her feet. Rubbing her eyes, she said, "What is it, Mama?"

Lily turned quickly. "Go back in the bedroom, Patty Ruth. Some men are riding toward the house."

"But, Mama—"

"Back in the bedroom . . . now," she said, pointing. Reluctantly the dark-haired little girl complied.

The horsemen were now at the porch. Lily stood to the right of the window, Charlie to the left.

"Hello the house!" a heavy voice called. Lily eyed them from the window's edge.

"Recognize 'em?" Charlie whispered.

"No. They're dressed too good to be saddle tramps. I doubt they're Curry's men. You keep an eye on them, Charlie."

Lacy nodded.

Lily slid the bolt back as the voice called again, "Hello the house!"

Lily pulled the door open and stepped onto the

porch. The buffalo gun was cradled in her arm. Her face was grim.

"Good mornin', ma'am," said the man whose horse stood closest to the porch. He was a stout man, thick in the shoulders and chest. His face was solid, with deep-set eyes. He wore a heavy mustache which was flecked with gray, as were his temples and sideburns. Lily judged him to be about fifty.

The other man was in his middle twenties. In contrast to the thick build of the older man, he was lean and slender. He was clean-shaven and had a winsome smile.

Neither man had made any move to dismount.

Touching the brim of his hat, the older man said, "I'm United States Marshal Logan Tanner, ma'am." Turning in the saddle, he nodded at his partner and said, "This is Deputy Tim Redmon."

Redmon touched his hat and smiled broadly. "Howdy-do, ma'am," he said warmly.

Lily managed a smile as she squinted against the morning sun. Relaxing the Sharps, she said, "You will forgive my air of apparent unfriendliness, gentlemen, but we've had much trouble of late." Directing her statement at Tanner, she said, "Would you like to get down and come in, Marshal? I'm Lily Dolan."

Both men dismounted to the sound of creaking leather. Each loosened his horse's cinch and wrapped his reins around the short hitching rail near the porch.

Approaching the porch, Logan Tanner said, "We're from the office in Raton, ma'am. On our way to Welcome."

Lily's eyes brightened. "You *are*?"

"Yes'm. We left Durango before sunup. Were gonna stop and cook breakfast just back the road apiece when we saw your chimney smoke. We decided we might see if we could buy a hot breakfast from you." Tanner hesitated briefly. "Your husband is not here?"

Charlie Lacy stepped into the doorway. "Howdy, Marshal," he said smiling. Moving into the sunlight, he extended his bony hand. "Don't shake it too hard, sir, I'm bandaged up a leetle. You can tell by lookin', I'm not the lady's husband."

Tanner's meaty hand squeezed the slender hand gently.

Redmon stepped forward and followed suit.

"I'm shotgunner on the Fargo stage that runs this route," Charlie said advisedly. "Name's Lacy. Charlie Lacy."

Tanner's face filled with a broad smile. "Just the man we're lookin' for," he blurted, looking at Redmon. "And what about Tally?"

A cloud shadowed Lacy's leathery face. "He's dead, Marshal."

"What about Wilford Lewis?" Tanner asked quickly.

"Dead too. Both of 'em's buried right out there behind that barn," Charlie said, gesturing toward the corral.

"Your office contacted us," said Tanner. "Told us the stage was due back in Durango. Said they feared somethin' bad had happened."

"It did, sir. It did," Lacy answered, nodding his head.

"Why don't you come on in, Marshal?" Lily asked. "I'll pour you some coffee, and you can sip that while I fix you some breakfast."

Tanner nodded and followed Lily through the door. Tim Redmon went next. Charlie brought up the rear. As they scooted the chairs and arranged themselves around the table, Lacy said, "I know your name, Marshal. You haven't been with the Raton office real long, have you?"

Logan Tanner smiled. "No. Only about three months. I was town marshal over in Holbrook, Arizona, before that. Got my government appointment about four months ago and moved over to Raton."

Over the succulent breakfast prepared by Lily Dolan, Marshal Logan Tanner learned of the trouble with Mel Curry, the disappearance of Tom Dolan and Bill Rice . . . and the attack on the stagecoach which left it at the cliff bottom. During the course of the story, told intermittently by Lily and the shotgunner, reference was made to the man who had shot the outlaws who jumped the stage, had whipped Mel Curry, and had volunteered to ride to Welcome.

At one point Logan Tanner said, "You've told me much of this 'Dan.' What is his last name?"

Lily answered quickly, "Colt."

Tanner pulled his face tight and almost choked on a buttered biscuit. "*Colt?*"

"Yes," Lily smiled, "and a fine man if there ever was one."

Tanner wiped his mouth with the back of his hand. His eyes were bulging. "Is he real tall?"

"Yes," Lily said softly.

"Blond?"

"Mm-hmm."

The Dolan children were eating at a tall wooden box next to the cupboard. Danny Dolan spoke up, "Yeah! And he has great big muscles, too!"

"Danny!" Lily said, eyeing the youngster. "Children—"

"Should be seen and not heard," the boy finished for her. "Sorry, ma'am," he added, dipping his chin.

Marshal Logan Tanner adjusted himself in the chair. After clearing his throat twice he frowned and said, "Mrs. Dolan, I hate to tell you this, but your Dan Colt is not Dan Colt, he's—"

"You're going to tell me he is Dave Sundeen, the outlaw," Lily said with a toss of her head.

"Escaped convict too," Tanner added emphatically.

Lily met Tanner's gaze directly. "You're wrong,

Marshal. He told me all about the confusion in Holbrook. The arrest. The trial. You're the one who sent him up."

Tanner felt his face flush. "Yes, ma'am." He was uncomfortable under her gaze. "I was just doing my duty. The jury convicted him."

"That young fella jist couldn't be an outlaw, Marshal," Charlie Lacy said with conviction. Shaking his head, he said, "Hard to believe a nice young fella like that could have a identical twin who is bad."

"That's just it, Lacy," Tanner said, easing back in his chair. "There is no evidence of this twin. Dave Sundeen is a liar and a bad case. He broke out of Yuma. Takes some mean thinking to do that."

"*Dan Colt* left Yuma so he could find *Dave Sundeen*," said Lily, with heavy emphasis on the names.

"If he was a outlaw, why did he jump in and help the Fargo stage? Tell me that, will yuh?" Lacy asked indignantly.

"Wanted it for himself," Tanner answered dryly.

"Why did he bother to save my life? Do you know he had to fight off a wolf to do it? Got hisself bit good and scratched up too. Outlaws don't care about other people, Marshal. I tell you—"

"Charlie, it's plain to see that Mr. Tanner has his mind made up about Dan," Lily interrupted. "He does not know Dan as we do. There's no sense in having a heated dispute. We can only hope that one day Dan can capture his twin and rub his nose against Mr. Tanner's."

Lily's eyes were like coals of fire. Tanner felt like they were reading his soul. There was a smile on her lips as she spoke. The smile did not reach her eyes.

"You said you were going to Welcome, Marshal."

"Yes'm," Tanner said, adjusting his weight in the chair. "Marshal Lewis was on his way to investigate some trouble that Welcome's marshal was having. No word had come from him, so we were sent to check out the stage disappearance and to find Lewis."

Danny Dolan had left his place at the tall box and now stood beside Logan Tanner. The big man turned to look at him.

Danny squinted his eyes and said, "I bet Dan could whip you with one arm tied behind him."

Lily tried to hide a furtive smile. "Danny, you go to the bedroom," she said firmly, wishing she could hug him.

The lad made his way to the bedroom door, then turned and said, "When I grow up, I'm gonna be just like Dan Colt!" Then he disappeared.

Logan Tanner stood up and reached for his hat. Tim Redmon followed suit. Tanner spoke. "How much do we owe you for the breakfast, Mrs. Dolan?"

"Absolutely nothing, Marshal. Let it be my token of good will. Though we differ in our opinions on Danny's hero, I know you are a lawman doing your duty."

Tanner donned his hat. "Thank you, ma'am. We'll be back as soon as we can. I hope we can return with your husband and not bad news."

"Thank you, Marshal," said Lily.

Tightening up the cinches, the two lawmen swung aboard their horses. Lily and Charlie stood on the porch. The air had a definite touch of spring. The warm rays of the sun felt good.

As Logan Tanner settled in the saddle, he pulled a pocketwatch from his vest and noted that it was nine o'clock. Touching the brim of his hat, he said, "Thanks again for the breakfast, ma'am. See you soon."

Lily nodded.

"Lacy," Tanner said, dipping his chin.

"Marshal," replied Lacy, doing the same.

Just before reigning his horse circular fashion, Tanner spied the face of Patty Ruth Dolan in the window. She was looking straight at him. Her nose was crinkled and her tongue was extended full length.

As the two riders evaporated into the trees where the road curved as it wended its way northward, Lily Dolan said, "Charlie, I always give the children a Sunday school lesson on Sunday morning. Would you like to sit in?"

Lacy's face took on the form of a dried prune. Lily's eyes read the expression, and Charlie suddenly let a broad grin capture his countenance. "Er . . . ah . . . sure, Miss Lily. Sure."

After the Sunday school lesson Lily began cleaning the breakfast table, and Patty Ruth pitched in to help.

"Sure glad that's a woman's job," said Lacy with a sigh.

"Me too!" said Danny.

"How would you two men like to go out and fork some hay for the horses?" Lily asked pleasantly. "Think you could handle a pitchfork, Charlie?"

"You betcha," said the leather-faced shotgunner. "I may be a mite slow at it, but I'll get it done."

"Let's go, Charlie," Danny said, charging the door.

"Put your jacket on, Danny," Lily commanded. "It's still a little cool out there."

Danny hotfooted it into the bedroom and quickly emerged, looping the jacket over his arms. He paused before his mother and lifted his hands upward. Lily bent down and kissed him. A serious look formed on his face. "Mama, Daddy's gonna be all right. I just know it. Dan Colt said he would bring him back. He'll do it, Mama."

Tears welled up in Lily's dark eyes. "Sure he will, honey." She wished she believed it.

The door closed behind the two men. Lily returned to her dishes, wiping tears from her face. Patty Ruth dried the dishes as her mother washed them.

Without looking toward Lily, she said with emotion, "Mama, I don't think Daddy's ever coming back. I think he's—" She burst into tears. Lily held her close and they wept together.

At first it sounded like distant thunder. Lily lifted her head and listened carefully. It was a low, rumbling sound. A vibration set up under their feet. Dishes tinkled on the shelves.

"What is it, Mama?" Patty Ruth asked, her voice trembling.

Lily spun around and ran to the door. She stepped out on the porch and looked toward the barn. Charging through the open area between the corral and a thick stand of trees was a thundering herd of cattle. "*Stampede!*" she shouted.

Suddenly her line of sight fell on Danny. He was playing beside the water trough next to the corral fence. The stampeding herd was bearing down on the boy.

Lily screamed his name. There was no way she could reach him ahead of the frightened herd. The front line of cattle was less than forty yards from the boy, who now saw them coming and stood frozen in his tracks.

The terrified mother saw Charlie Lacy bound from the barn door, running headlong for the boy. He gathered him up into his arms just as the herd struck.

Lily screamed as she saw them go down. The pole fence was cracking and collapsing in the wake of the bawling, panicking herd. The horses inside the barn were whinnying with fear.

As the cattle pounded past the barn, they collided with the shed which held the buckboard. It collapsed with a roar. The three remaining outbuildings went down. Then something seemed to turn the charging animals toward the house.

Lily ran off the porch toward Danny without realizing it. Suddenly she became aware of her own danger.

Whirling, she darted for the house. Patty Ruth was standing on the porch, numb with terror. In one sweeping move the mother picked her up and plunged through the door. They landed in a heap on the kitchen floor.

All at once the herd struck the porch. It peeled off the house like dried bark from a tree. Lily had not closed the door. The thunderous roar of pounding hoofs boomed in their ears. Patty Ruth shrieked as the building shook. Articles all over the house were falling to the floor.

Suddenly the din was moving away. The last of the cattle splashed across the swollen stream, and within seconds the sound of thundering hoofs died away.

Lily rose to her knees. Patty Ruth clung to her, trembling. She wept as Lily held her tight and said soothingly, "It's all over now, honey. Mama's got to go see about Danny and Charlie."

"Don't leave me, Mama!" the terrified child cried.

"Patty Ruth, I've got to go to Danny. You'll be safe here in the house."

"No, please! Let me go with you!"

Lily knew she could not allow the child to see what the stampeding cattle had left of her little brother, or of Charlie Lacy. It would be a sight Patty Ruth would never forget. She must not see it. Holding her close for several minutes, the mother was able to calm her down and get her to agree. Remaining in the house was best.

Lily Dolan lifted herself to a standing position. For a moment she thought her legs would collapse. Little by little she made her way to the door. She leaned against the jamb until her legs gathered strength.

The porch was a shambles. The roof had caved in and lay in a heap amongst the rubble. Lily stepped off the threshold and threaded her way through the debris. Her heart pounded in her breast like a triphammer as she edged her way reluctantly toward the demolished corral. She felt numb all over.

Her eyes fell on the battered body of the Wells Fargo shotgunner. She stopped in her tracks. Her hand flew to her mouth. For a moment a wave of nausea swept over her. Closing both eyes, she drew a deep breath. As the nausea passed, she opened her eyes and moved closer. *Danny! Where's Danny?* The boy was nowhere in sight.

The lifeless body of Charlie Lacy lay in a crumpled heap, next to the water trough. His clothing was torn and soaked with blood.

Only as Lily moved close enough to stand over Lacy's body did she see Danny. He was lying in the trough in two inches of water. Lily gasped. He was breathing! Unconscious, but *breathing!*

A piteous cry escaped her lips as she gently picked him up. His arms and legs dangled lifelessly as she carried him to the house.

It was clear now what had happened. When Charlie saw the charging cattle bearing down on Danny, he knew there was one chance to save the boy. The cattle would probably veer around the stone trough. If he could deposit the boy into it, he had a chance to survive the stampede. There was not enough time to get Danny in the trough and return to safety. Charlie had not hesitated. He had willingly given his life to save Danny Dolan.

Leaving their horses in the protective thicket of the trees, Mel Curry's riders crept to the edge of the clearing. Ralph Dunbar clucked his tongue and shook his head. "Boy, is that corral a mess! Sheds are done for too," he said with a chuckle.

"Ralph! Look!" exclaimed one of the riders. "Isn't that a man lyin' there by the water trough?"

Several voices agreed that it was.

Dunbar pushed his hat back and shaded his eyes,

studying the lifeless figure on the ground. Suddenly a string of curse words escaped his lips. "I told the boss somebody could get killed. It's Tom Dolan."

An unhealthy murmur swept through the crowd of Curry cowhands. "We never meant to kill nobody, Ralph," one of them blurted.

"Hold it!" came another voice. "The woman's leavin' the house."

The group huddled amongst the trees and watched Lily Dolan as she slowly made her way toward the dead man. Drawing near, she paused, cupping her hand over her mouth.

One of the riders let out a moan.

As Lily lifted Danny from the water trough, another rider gasped, "Oh, dear God, what have we done?"

"We killed that little kid," another said, dropping his hat to the ground.

Ralph Dunbar laid his head against a white-barked aspen. He was sick to his stomach.

CHAPTER SEVENTEEN

As Logan Tanner and Tim Redmon began the twelve mile ride to Welcome, George Keighley unlocked the cell door.

"It's nine o'clock," Keighley said solemnly.

"Don't look so worried," Dan Colt said, patting his shoulder. "With all that breakfast you brought me, I could wrestle a grizzly."

Tate Landry had left a few minutes before nine. At the moment Colt and Keighley were alone. As they entered the office, Keighley said, "Dan, all the men were alerted before midnight. They were disappointed, but the fight is still in 'em."

A faint smile tugged at Dan's lips. "Good. We'll come out of this thing yet."

As Dan stepped toward the door, Keighley's heavy hand fell on his shoulder. The tall man turned and their eyes met. "Before you go out there," Keighley said huskily, "I want you to know that I'm sorry I ever got mixed up with Waite. However it goes, I'll be pullin' for you. And Dan . . ."

"Yeah?"

"If Waite is too much for you and—well . . . if he should win . . . I want you to know that I'm gonna get the ammunition from the gun shop and help these people shake loose of Waite."

A smile spread across Dan's face, lifting his ears. He extended his hand to Keighley. They gripped each other for a brief moment, then stepped out on the boardwalk.

A crowd was gathered in front of the Empire Saloon. Kyle Waite had forced the entire populace of the town, minus the hostages, to gather as spectators. As yet Waite had not appeared. His men stood on the edge of the crowd, hands on their gun butts.

Drawing near, Dan saw Annie Rankin. Standing next to Flora Bailey, she looked bigger than ever. Presently Nellie Rice sided in next to the Bailey woman.

Standing between Lippy Norgren and Alfredo Saldivar was Louie Stokes. Some color had returned to Louie's face. A fresh bandage circled his head. Ed Sorenson's bald pate glistened in the sunlight as he conversed with a man whose name Dan did not know.

The crowd was centered in the muddy street, arranged in a wide circle. The sun was showing signs of making it a warm day.

George Keighley stepped ahead of the tall man and parted the crowd. Moving into the circle, Dan looked at Nellie Rice and grinned. The small woman forced a feeble smile. Fear was written on her face.

By pure accident Dan's gaze fell on the face of Louie Stokes. The youth's eyes flared with blood-red hatred. His upper lip tightened against his teeth.

Suddenly the door of the Empire opened, and Tate Landry appeared. Waite's absence until this moment was nothing short of cheap theatrics. He wanted to make a singular, dynamic appearance. Some twenty seconds behind Landry the big man emerged through the door. The members of the gang cheered. All except George Keighley. No one seemed to notice.

Elbowing his way through the outer fringe of the crowd, Landry cleared the way for Waite. The outlaw leader's formidable frame seemed to fill the circle. He stopped ten feet from his intended victim, his big head lurching, and focused his eyes on Dan's face. "You ready for your Sunday school lesson, sonny?"

Dan Colt fixed his ice-water eyes on Waite's crooked nose. "Any time you are, daddy."

The huge man lifted his voice. "I want all of you people to see what happens to a man jack who guns down my men, then tries to muscle in on my operation. When I'm through with him, he'll be a lifeless pile of pulp. You better all get this Sunday school lesson and get it good!" Turning his head in both directions, he said, "I don't want nobody buttin' in. You hear? If he happens to get in a good lick a time or two before I finish him, you men stay out of it. He's all mine. Understand?"

Waite's dark eyes sought out the face of each of his men. His gaze held them till each man nodded.

Without warning Louie Stokes snatched Lippy Norgren's gun from its holster and swung it on Dan Colt, stepping into the circle. "Oh, no you don't, Waite!" he screeched. "He killed Huey! I'm gonna kill him!" The cylinder turned as he thumbed back the hammer.

Dan leaped sideways. The crowd in Louie's line of fire began to disperse. A Colt .45 roared from the edge of the crowd. Louie Stokes buckled. His eyes registered shock. In one brief spasm he flopped on his back, coughed once, and died. A crimson stain gathered around the fresh hole in his shirt. His sightless eyes stared toward the blue Colorado sky.

Every eye sped to the smoking revolver in George Keighley's hand.

Kyle Waite motioned toward the corpse. "Couple you men get that chunk of garbage outta here."

Lippy Norgren retrieved his gun from Louie's dead fingers. Easing the hammer into place, he wiped mud off the barrel and dropped it in his holster.

Waite looked at George Keighley. "Good goin',

George. Little snip nearly deprived me of teachin' my Sunday school lesson today."

Keighley's eyes met Dan's. Keighley read the gratitude in the tall man's expression. If there had been any doubt in Colt's mind about George Keighley, it was gone now.

The crowd reassembled under the prodding of Waite's men. Dan cast a glance at Nellie Rice. Her face was pale and pinched. She was leaning on Annie Rankin.

"Let's get on with the lesson!" Kyle Waite's voice boomed.

The enormous man peeled off his shirt, exposing a deep, rounded chest, matted with coarse black hair. His arms were as thick as an average man's thighs. Laying his hands against his chest, he worked his elbows in circular fashion. Dan knew this was more show than warm-up.

The tall blond man removed his shirt quietly. Almost without thinking Nellie Rice extended her hand to receive it. He nodded in appreciation.

Dan Colt worked his arms, loosening the shoulder joints. Years of hard work had formed him perfectly. In contrast to Kyle Waite's thick middle, the younger man's broad shoulders tapered from a muscular chest to a hard, slim waist. As he moved his arms, the muscles in his back corded in a display of veiled power.

Annie Rankin eyed his heavy-veined biceps and lifted her gaze to his squared jaw and the blond locks bouncing on his finely sculptured forehead. "Some specimen of a man," she whispered to Nellie Rice.

Sloping his massive shoulders, Kyle Waite roared, "All right, sonny. Class is in session." Going into a crouch, he balled his huge fists and scowled heavily.

The icy fear that hung in the air was a tangible thing. It seeped through the crowd like a heavy mist.

Feeling deep respect for the man's size and obvious

power, Dan Colt allowed himself no fear. As Waite moved in like a runaway freight train, Dan knew he must unload quickly on the giant's vulnerable spot.

Death leered at Dan Colt through Kyle Waite's eyes.

Nimbly Dan dodged the pumping fists of the heavier man. Waite wheeled, slightly off balance. Dan saw his opening. He smashed Waite in the nose with a hissing right fist. It was quick, brutal, and savage. Waite staggered slightly, surprise registered on his face. Finding the nose momentarily unguarded, Dan hit it again, viciously.

Kyle Waite's surprise turned to anger. His eyes watered as he swore at Dan, emanating a deep-down rage. He charged like an angry bull. Dan set his feet to dodge, but the slippery mud gave way, and Waite caught him full-force in the stomach with a hard blow. Breath whooshed from Dan Colt's mouth. The big fist doubled him over, and Waite clubbed him on the back of the neck. The force of the blow flattened him in the mud.

Waite aimed for him with his knees, dropping down with his full weight. Colt rolled rapidly, and Waite hit the mud hard.

Dan flipped to his feet, still partially stunned from the punch in the stomach. Just as the giant gained his feet, Colt rushed in and peppered the big nose with three straight lefts. Waite stumbled momentarily but kept on coming. He threw a punch that caught Dan's shoulder, spinning him partially. Dan corrected the spin and rebounded with a violent right to Waite's jaw. It landed solidly. Dan felt it all the way from his fist to the bottom of his right foot. It slowed the big beast only momentarily.

Before Dan could step back and plant himself, Waite caught him on the forehead with a hard left, and Dan went down. Lights exploded inside his head. He saw the horrified face of Nellie Rice hovering over him as he landed in the mud. Kyle Waite's heavy boot caught him in the ribs and set them on fire. The kick unbalanced the big man on the slick surface. He stumbled backward.

Dan took advantage of the brief reprieve and got on his feet. His heart was pounding against his burning ribs, his mouth making a whistling sound as he gasped for air. Waite was coming again, like a bull elephant. Dan knew he could not continue to withstand the big man's onslaughts. There was no way he could stand toe to toe and trade punches. The man was too big, too strong. He had to keep away and work on the nose, which was now showing a trickle of blood.

The massive man charged again with a wild yell, head down, fists pumping. Again the softness beneath Dan's feet worked against him, and he was unable to dodge. Waite's shoulder slammed his hip, and the two men rolled in the mud, fists flailing.

The battle was savage and raw. Waite's men cheered their leader. One by one the people of Welcome found the courage to yell for Dan Colt.

When they got to their feet, Colt shot a hard fist to his opponent's nose. Almost instantly he caught one of Waite's fists along the side of his head. It was a glancing blow, but it stung his ear. Again Dan chopped the big man's nose. Waite shook his head and made a quick swipe at his hairy upper lip. The blood was flowing freely now.

The momentary attention to the blood cost him two more slamming punches on the nose. Waite stumbled forward, missing a wild swing. Dan retreated, sucking hard for air. His mouth was dry as a sand pit. His ribs were on fire and his stomach pained horribly.

Rushing the huge monster again, he planted two more stiff punches on the swollen nose. Another punch caught Dan on the mouth and instantly he tasted blood. The pain quickened his senses and he ducked another punch.

Retaliating by sheer reflex, born of previous fights, the tall man landed another smashing blow to Kyle Waite's nose. Waite was stunned momentarily, and Colt brought a right cross from outer space, catching the bearded man on the socket of the left jaw. His eyes glazed, and Dan hit him another straight punch on the blood-smeared nose.

Wildly Waite lunged forward, tackling the blond man. As they rolled in the mud amidst the shouting crowd, Dan felt a big thumb trying to gouge his left eye. Blindly he groped for the thumb with his mouth, found it and bit down with all the strength in his jaw. Waite howled and cursed. Dan let go of the thumb and spit blood. Some was his own. Most was Waite's.

Again they were on their feet. Waite was missing punches now, and Dan knew the battered nose was having its effect. As a big meaty fist whistled past his ear, he chopped the nose again with his left, following with another hard right to the jaw. Kyle Waite went down. Lippy Norgren stepped in to help him up. Annie Rankin, anger flushing her face, leaped in and swung a looping punch. It caught Norgren on the temple, and he dropped like a sickled weed. She sank her big fingers into his shirt and dragged him from the circle. "Mr. Waite said no interference," she rasped. The crowd laughed. Even some of Waite's men joined in the laughter.

George Keighley watched with intensity. No man had ever lasted this long against the formidable giant. Waite's strength was ebbing, and the blond man's battle plan was working.

Dan Colt took the brief respite offered by the Norgren-Rankin episode to catch his breath. Under different circumstances he would have had a good laugh at Annie's adept handling of Lippy Norgren. Maybe he could laugh about it later.

Kyle Waite was on his feet, his heart pounding violently, his breath burning his lungs. Blood was pouring from both nostrils. Throwing caution aside and relying on his brute strength, he charged the younger man again.

Waite was like a mortally wounded wild beast. Dan tagged him with a solid blow to the mouth but caught another big fist on the jaw. He felt his knees give, and suddenly Waite was on top of him. Blood from his nose splattered Dan's face. The massive man was trying to choke him. He felt as big as a mountain, his weight pinning Dan to the earth.

Dan tried to spring himself loose, but Waite was too heavy. His huge thumbs were pressing down on Dan's windpipe. Nellie Rice was screaming. Annie Rankin was shouting something Dan could not understand.

Clawing at Waite's hands, he could not break the viselike grip on his throat. Thinking fast, he reached up and closed his thumb and forefinger on the big man's nose and twisted it violently. When he felt the cartilage snap, he knew the nose was broken. Savagely Dan wrung the nose. Sticky red liquid covered his hand.

Gradually Waite's grip on Dan Colt's throat lessened. With a piercing cry, he let go of the throat and grabbed Dan's hand. For a moment Waite lost his balance, and the lithe Dan Colt was out from under him. Dan's legs revolted when he stood up but finally stiffened to hold him.

Kyle Waite groped his way to his feet. His breathing was like the rattle of dry weeds in an autumn wind. Blood bubbled from his nose.

Dan would not give him time to fortify himself. He closed in, anger burning his veins like raw whisky.

The big man's face was beet-red, his massive chest

heaving, blood dripping from his beard. Dan smashed the nose again. Waite staggered, his legs rubbery. The blow had blurred his vision. He swung wildly. Tate Landry shouted something Waite never heard.

Dan summoned every ounce of his remaining strength, firmly planted his feet, and sledge-hammered his right fist into Waite's jaw socket. The big man's feet flew upward from the impact of the blow, and his immense frame slammed the ground with an earth-shaking thud. Kyle Waite did not move. He was out cold. The crowd cheered. Waite's men drew their guns.

Immediately Tate Landry threw his gun on Dan Colt, who stood on wobbly legs, shoulders drooped.

"Hold it right there, mister!" Landry barked. Dan eyed him warily. Tate looked at George Keighley. "George, take him back to the jail. Hold him there till you hear from me."

Keighley pointed his gun at Colt. Nellie Rice stepped forward and handed the weary man his shirt. He was a pitiful sight. Mud was caked all over him, mingled with blood, most of which was Kyle Waite's. The scratches from his encounter with the wolf were bleeding, as was the bruise on his cheekbone. The wolf bite on his left arm had reopened also. His blond hair was matted with mud and blood and clung closely to his head.

Nellie looked at him with compassion. "I'm proud of you, Dan," she said softly.

Two of Waite's men had compelled Flora Bailey to kneel in the mud and see to Kyle Waite. The big man had not yet regained consciousness.

"Let's go, Dan," said George Keighley sharply, disguising his real feelings.

The crowd was dispersing. Landry, who was standing over his conquered hero, turned and approached Dan Colt. Drawing his lips in a thin line, he hissed,

"You're a dead man, mister. When he wakes up, he'll have your hide stretched on the nearest tree."

Dan fixed his hard blue stare on Landry's face and said nothing.

"If you know how to pray, you'd better get started," Landry said. His voice was strident. "You're as good as dead." He wheeled and returned to his fallen leader.

As Dan and George Keighley started toward the jail, Nellie Rice walked alongside Keighley. "Mr. Keighley," she said pleadingly, "Dan's wounds need care. Would you let me—"

"Ma'am, if there's time, I'll see he gets a bath and his wounds are cared for," Keighley said kindly. "But when Waite comes out of it, only God can stop him from killing Colt."

"Isn't there something you can do?" she asked, keeping pace.

"It'd be me against the whole gang, ma'am. I'm only one man."

"You could give Dan his guns. Then there would be two of you."

"I thought about that," said Keighley, "but we would still be outnumbered seventeen to two."

"Then give him his guns and let him go." Nellie's voice wavered.

"I would even do that, ma'am, but I won't get the chance. If you'll look behind you, you'll see two men following us. Landry is taking no chances."

Tears filled Nellie's eyes. She spoke to Colt. "Dan, what are we going to do?"

"We're going to break Waite, Nellie," the tall man said confidently. "Don't give up. I'm not dead yet."

George Keighley unlocked the office door. The two men dispatched by Tate Landry caught up with them when they stopped.

Dan turned and looked at Nellie. "You go on back

to the hotel. I'll be all right." He managed a weak smile. "Thank you for your concern."

Nellie was left standing on the boardwalk. The four men entered the marshal's office, and the door closed behind them.

It was just past noon when Dan Colt stepped out of the galvanized tub. George Keighley had supplied him with hot water, soap, and a towel. The tub was in the open space just outside the cell door.

Kyle Waite's two henchmen loitered in the office.

Gingerly Dan patted the towel over his bruised body. He wondered if any ribs were broken. It hurt plenty to breathe.

The two men were expressing concern that they had heard nothing as to Kyle Waite's condition.

Keighley had procured some salve for Dan to dress his wounds. It was designed for healing saddle and harness sores on horses. It smelled strong and burned like molten lava as he applied it to the open wounds.

Dan pulled on his muddy pants, wishing for clean ones. He slipped into his boots and buttoned his shirt. His ribs were killing him.

Heavy footsteps sounded on the boardwalk, and the outer door came open. Dan heard Tate Landry's voice. "George, get the blue-eyed wonder and bring him outside."

"What's going on?" Keighley asked nervously.

"The boss was out cold for nearly half an hour. He's lost a lot of blood and he's weak. But he's like a wounded tiger. He wants to kill him right now."

"What's he gonna do?" one of the two men asked.

"Tie him to the hitching rail in front of the Empire and be a one-man firing squad."

Keighley said something Dan could not make out.

Landry swore and said, "Get him, George. Now."

Escorted by Keighley and the other two, Dan stepped out into the bright sunlight. As they approached the Empire, several of Waite's men were gathered like vultures, ready to pounce on a piece of dead meat. Kyle Waite was seated in the street on a straight-backed chair, holding a Winchester .44. His face was a puffy mass. Cotton had been stuffed into both nostrils. The nose was swollen three times its normal size.

Tate Landry left Waite's side, carrying a length of rope. The two men with Keighley grasped the tall man and pinned him to the hitching rail. Waite sat forty feet away, facing the intended victim. As Dan was being tied securely, Kyle Waite glared at him, red daggers of rage in his puffy eyes.

None of Welcome's citizens were allowed on the street. Some peered through windows, looking on in horror.

As Landry and the other men stepped away, Waite snarled and said, "Nobody shames me and lives. You die!"

George Keighley moved toward Waite. "Wait a minute, Kyle," he shouted. "Let me talk to you!"

"Shut up, George," Waite snapped, levering a shell into the chamber.

In the excitement no one had noticed the two riders approach.

"Hold it right there!" a big voice roared.

Every eye swept toward the intruder. Two men sat astride two horses. Both of them with badges on their vests, glistening in the sunlight. One of the lawmen was heavily built with a thick mustache. The other was slender and clean shaven.

The slender man was pointing his gun at Kyle Waite.

Dan found the heavy man's face with his gaze. It was *Logan Tanner*!

CHAPTER EIGHTEEN

Logan Tanner looked at Dan Colt. "Hello, Sundeen," he said. Tanner's face was without expression.

Dan did not answer. To do so would weaken his case that he was not Dave Sundeen.

Tanner swung his line of sight to Kyle Waite. The latter was glaring at Tim Redmon, who held his gun steadily on him. Redmon's horse blew.

"What's going on here?" Tanner demanded coarsely.

Kyle Waite started to speak.

Tate Landry, standing next to Waite, spoke up. "Just teaching this man a lesson, Marshal," he said, pointing to Dan Colt. "He got a little out of line." Landry chuckled uneasily. "We weren't really going to shoot him."

Logan Tanner reached in his pocket and produced a pocket knife. Tossing it to Landry, he said, "Cut him loose. He's going with me."

Kyle Waite's eyes bulged. With a thick-tongued sound, he said loudly, "Where you takin' him?"

"He's an escaped convict. Doing time for gunning me down in Holbrook, Arizona."

Kyle Waite's brain was spinning. The vengeance he held against Dan Colt was a suppressed ball of fire in his chest. He deeply wanted the satisfaction of blowing him out of this world. On the other hand, his greatest passion was for gold. It was his cankerous greed that had driven him to murder Clyde Tutor and take over the mine. That same irresponsible greed had carried him to the point of forcing men into slavery and besieging a quiet and peaceful town.

Waite knew his time to milk the mine of its wealth was limited. As his thoughts collected, he decided to let the lawmen take their prisoner and be gone. The army would be riding in next, if these men were detained long. Waite could not afford that.

Tim Redmon still held his gun on Waite. Tanner's gun was yet in its holster.

Kyle Waite opened his mouth to tell them they could take their prisoner and leave. Suddenly from across the street a gun roared, and Redmon jerked from the impact of the bullet. Before the slender deputy hit the ground, Tanner drew and fired at the man who had shot Redmon. Tanner's bullet seared the man's shoulder. Before he could fire another shot, a dozen guns were leveled at him.

"Hold it right there, Marshal!" It was Tate Landry's voice.

Tanner checked himself.

"Drop it, Marshal," Landry snapped. Tanner's gun made a soft plopping sound as it struck the mud. "Climb down," Landry commanded.

Saddle leather creaked as Logan Tanner dismounted.

Kyle Waite twisted on his chair to look at the man the marshal had winged. The look of hot steel touched the outlaw leader's puffy eyes.

Logan Tanner ignored Landry's gun, along with the others directed toward him. He walked around his horse and knelt down beside Tim Redmon. The slender deputy was dead.

Waite glared at Lippy Norgren, who was holding his bleeding shoulder. Waite's fury bolted strength through his body. He stood up, rifle in hand. Swaying as he walked toward Norgren, he cursed the man violently. "Where's your good sense, Norgren?" he yelled. "We'd have been rid of 'em in a little while. Now you've botched it up!"

Norgren saw the rage in Waite's battered face. "But, boss, I—" The little man never finished. Waite fired the Winchester from hip level. The bullet struck Norgren in the heart. He was dead before he hit the ground.

Logan Tanner erected himself and glared at Tate Landry, who still held him at gunpoint. He swore vehemently. "What is going on here?" he bellowed.

Landry turned toward Kyle Waite, who was being helped back to his chair. "Shall I tell him, boss?"

Waite slumped into the chair. Blood had soaked through the cotton in his nose and was finding its way into his mustache. He took a deep breath and spoke through swollen lips. "Yeah. Go ahead, Tate. It'll give me time to think what to do next. Can't let him go now, anyway."

Tanner's ears pricked up. His eyes centered on Landry's face. "Tate?" The U.S. marshal squinted his eyes. "Are you *Tate Landry*?"

A definite sneer formed on Landry's face. "Heard of me, eh, Marshal?"

"You've lasted longer than most of them. How long you been fanning leather now? Three, four years?"

"'Bout that long," Landry said, his face now drawn tight. "I'm quick, Marshal. Mighty quick. I plan to last a lot longer."

"What are you doing here, in this one-horse town? Not much to hire your gun out for here."

"That's all in the story, Marshal. Gold. Pure gold."

Tanner's heavy eyebrows arched.

Dan Colt tried to readjust himself into a more comfortable position against the hitching rail as Tate Landry told Logan Tanner of the gold mine and Welcome's present plight.

When Landry finished, Tanner looked at Redmon's

corpse and shook his head. Slowly lifting his gaze to Kyle Waite, he said grimly, "Now what?"

"Looks like you gotta die, lawman. I ain't left with no choice since that idiot killed your deputy. Can't let you just ride out of here, can I?"

Tanner cast a sidelong glance at Dan Colt.

"Tie him up with the yeller-haired dog," Waite snapped, levering a fresh shell into the chamber of his Winchester.

As Tate Landry guided Tanner toward the hitching rail, George Keighley approached Kyle Waite. "Boss," he said gravely, "you ain't thinking too clearly."

Waite flashed him a hard look. "What you talkin' about?"

"When the marshal and his deputy turn up missin', you can be sure the cavalry will be coming from Fort Lewis."

Waite scowled. "So you ain't tellin' me nuthin' I don't know."

"So we gotta shake loose all the gold we can in the next few days . . . four, or five at the most, right? Then we gotta hightail it outta here fast, right?"

Waite nodded with disdain.

"Well, take a look at those two," Keighley said, pointing at Colt and Tanner. "Them two huskies could dig a lot of gold in four, five days."

A light lit up in Kyle Waite's dull eyes. A smile eased its way across his swollen mouth. "Yeah. You're right, George. How many we got diggin' out there now? A dozen?"

Keighley looked at Landry, who was tying Tanner to the rail. Landry paused and nodded. "Yeah. There's twelve right now."

"Good! Couple more as husky as them two will make a big difference. We'll kill 'em just before we leave." Waite laughed. "That is unless we work 'em to death first!" He laughed again.

As Colt and Tanner were being untied, George Keighley convinced Waite to let him lock up the two men in the jail and feed them a good meal before transporting them to the mine. Fed well, they could work harder. Acceding to Keighley's request, Kyle Waite decided that he should put a good meal in his own belly. With the aid of two men he made his way toward the hotel.

Keighley retrieved Tanner's revolver from the muddy street. He gave orders to a couple of men to take the lawmen's horses to the livery. To a couple others he assigned the task of removing Redmon's body from the street.

Much to Keighley's dismay Tate Landry accompanied the procession to the jail. Keighley had a plan. It must be executed quickly. He had to share it with Colt and Tanner immediately.

Logan Tanner was forming a plan of his own. As the foursome made their way jailward, he spoke to Landry. "You think you're fast with a gun, huh? You ain't a drop in the bucket compared to Sundeen, here."

Dan gave Tanner a sour look. Keighley eyed Dan quizzically.

"Name's Colt," Dan said flatly.

Ignoring Dan's statement, Tanner continued. "I had a gun on him in Holbrook. Hammer back. He drew and cut me down before I could fire."

Dan Colt knew Tanner was describing his twin. He wondered if, when the day came that he found Dave, he would have to draw against him. If so, could he do it? And if he could, which twin was fastest?

George Keighley unlocked the office door.

"He'd make you look like January molasses, Landry," Tanner said with conviction.

"There ain't a man alive could do that," Landry said defensively.

"Dave Sundeen could." Tanner's voice was edged sharply. He saw a flinty spark touch Landry's eyes.

The quartet moved to the cell area. "You in number one, Marshal," Keighley said gesturing. "You in number two," he motioned to Dan. Both doors clanged shut.

Landry moved close to Tanner's door. The latter was standing close to the bars. "You're tryin' to goad me into a gunfight with blue eyes, here. It ain't gonna work. You have an ulterior motive behind it, and I'm smart enough to know it." His face drew tight. "But I'll tell you this, lawman. I can take your Dave Sundeen, here. I'm quick, man. Mighty quick.

"He's quicker," snapped Tanner. A sardonic mask formed on his weathered face. "And he's *deadly*." Their eyes locked in defiant agitation.

"Don't push me, lawman," Landry hissed, his breath hot. "It'll be you that'll square off with me."

"I want to know the truth," George Keighley rasped at Dan. "Are you Dan Colt, or Dave Sundeen?"

Landry wheeled. "*Dan Colt?* Whaddya mean, *Dan Colt?*"

"That's who I am," Dan said brusquely.

"*The* Dan Colt?" Landry asked, tilting his head.

"Yep."

"He's dead. Ambushers got him."

"Just hearsay. I hung up my guns. Went to ranching up in Wyoming."

"You're lyin'."

"Marshal Tanner thinks so too." Dan shot a cold stare toward the adjacent cell.

"We can't stand here jawin', Tate," George Keighley said quickly. "I'm taking his word he's Dan Colt. But we'd better get them fed and over to the mine before the boss gets through eating."

"Yep, we'd better," agreed Landry. "I'll have big

Annie slap something together and send one of the boys over with it. I gotta talk to Waite, anyway."

Keighley heaved a secret sigh of relief.

Landry turned to leave. He paused in the doorway. Looking over his shoulder, he said to Tanner, "Even if he is Dan Colt, I can take him." He chuckled. "Quick and deadly?" He chuckled louder. "I'm quicker and deadlier." With that, he was gone.

As soon as the outside door slammed shut, Keighley put the key in Dan's door and unlocked it. "C'mon. I'll get your guns for you."

Dan eased out of the cell and stopped.

"We've gotta work fast," George said, heading for the office. "It's now or never."

"Wait a minute, George," Dan said. "We can't just go at it blindly. We've got to organize."

"There isn't time."

"They'll cut us down, George. There's too many of them. We've got to get ammunition to the people."

Logan Tanner's puzzled face was pressed against the bars.

Keighley nodded. "Okay. How do you want to do it?"

"You go right now, while Waite's at the hotel, and get the key to the gun shop. We'll have to gamble that he won't look for it."

Keighley nodded again. "Uh-huh."

"How will we get to the mine?"

"In a wagon. Too easy to make a run for it if you're on a horse. One of the other men will drive the wagon. I'll ride along on my horse as escort. That's been the procedure."

"Good. You put my guns in your saddlebags and some extra shells. There's no time to clean Tanner's gun, so put in a .45 for him."

Tanner's tense face relaxed.

Keighley's countenance clouded. "But Dan. He'll put you back in prison if—"

"We need him, George. Not only that, but I'm trying to convince him that I'm me and not my twin. Get to Ed Sorenson. Tell him to spread the word fast." Dan turned to Tanner. "What time is it?"

Producing the watch from his vest, he said, "One ten."

Keighley checked his own watch. "Yep. One ten."

"All right," said Dan hurriedly. "Tell Sorenson we'll go at dawn tomorrow, just as we had planned for this morning. Same everything. You conk the guard at the barber shop as planned. The wagon wheel will be the signal as before."

"Okay."

"Can you get the key, alert Sorenson, and be back here by one thirty?"

"I'll try."

"Good. Tanner and I will need plenty of daylight after we get to the mine. We've got to have it in control before dark."

Keighley locked Dan back in his cell and disappeared through the door.

"You know I'll have to take you in when this is over." Tanner eyed him through the bars.

Dan's face was grim. "We'll have to see about that. Right now, this town has got to be freed."

"You get your guns, you gonna turn 'em on me?"

Dan smiled. "Even Dave Sundeen wouldn't do that."

Tanner pursed his lips. "Oh, yeah?"

"If he wanted you dead, you'd have been so that night in Holbrook."

Tanner was silent for several minutes. "You gonna shoot me to keep me from taking you in?"

"Nope. But I'll find a way to stop you. I can't track down my brother and prove his existence sitting in Yuma."

* * *

The sun was on the downward side of the western sky as Dan Colt and Logan Tanner sat in the bed of the wagon, watching George Keighley follow on his horse. Dan grimaced with every bump. His ribs felt like knives were stabbing his side.

The driver, Jim Feldman, was a man in his mid-forties. He had insisted that the prisoners be bound hand and foot for the ride to the mine. George Keighley had argued against it. He assured Feldman that he would watch them closely. Feldman had given in, with the solemn warning for Keighley to ride close.

Dan was thinking ahead as the wagon moved toward the mine. As it rounded a turn, he spotted the place on the mountain where he had wrestled with the man whose heart gave out.

Clutching his side, he shouted to the driver to stop. "I've got to rest up just a moment," he said. "These ribs are killing me."

Feldman pulled the wagon to a stop. Dan stood up in the wagon bed. Feldman was looking toward the mine. Bracing his feet, Dan said quietly, "Feldman."

The driver turned his head. A savage fist smashed his jaw. He rolled out of the seat and hit the ground hard. "Tie him up," Dan said to Keighley. "He'll come to shortly." Gingerly he climbed out of the wagon. "You wait here, George. Tanner and I will be back in a few minutes."

"Where you going?" Keighley asked, dismounting.

"Up that hill. We'll be right back. C'mon, Tanner."

Dan started up the steep grade, Tanner following. The latter was protesting the climb, to no avail.

Arriving at the spot where the squared wooden apparatus lay adjacent to the ground, Dan ran his line of sight up the slope just above it. "I thought I remembered correctly," he said aloud to himself.

Tanner was puffing heavily. "What are you talkin'

about?" he said, wiping his sweaty brow. He eyed the shaft covering. "What's that?"

"A special escape route from the mine. When we hit the camp, some of Waite's men may make a dash for the mine. There's no way we could follow them. This will be their hope of escape. We've got to plug it. See that boulder?" Dan pointed up the slope.

"Yeah," said Tanner, still breathing hard.

"Let's see if we can dislodge it and roll it over the shaft."

The two men climbed to where the boulder clung loosely to the slope. Dan gripped it firmly and rocked it a little.

"That thing'll weigh a ton," Tanner protested.

"Naw," said Dan. "I bet it doesn't weigh over a thousand pounds. C'mon, push."

Together the two got it wobbling. Presently the boulder rolled forward, scooted for a few feet, and landed heavily right on top of the covering. Wood cracked and splintered.

"That'll plug the hole," said Dan. "C'mon. It's easier going down."

Shortly Dan Colt was tying the thongs on his holster to his muscular thighs. Shaking his head as he tested his draw, he said, "Now I feel complete again."

Leaving Jim Feldman tied to the wagon, Colt, Tanner, and Keighley made their way to the camp on foot. Crouching behind a rock formation, the trio peered toward the yawning hole in the side of the mountain. The sound of the single jack echoed through the rock-walled enclosure.

"There'll be two guards just around these rocks," Keighley advised. "They're one short since that one had the heart failure. Three will be back in the mine with the prisoners. Usually the sixth man stayed close to the buildings. The cook is a prisoner."

"Best thing is to take out the two guards and catch the others as they come out of the mine," said Dan.

"Yeah," agreed Keighley. "These two here won't suspect a thing if I come meanderin' in. I'll tell them my horse went lame and make small talk. You two bop 'em. Each bed in the bunkhouse has leg irons chained to it. Prisoners are chained up at night. We can chain the guards in there if we can take 'em alive."

Colt and Tanner agreed. As Keighley stepped into the rock opening, Dan eyed the position of the sun. It had almost disappeared behind the western peaks. They must work fast.

George Keighley now had the attention of the two guards. He maneuvered them so their backs were toward the opening. The two big men moved up stealthily. There were two *whomp whomp* sounds and the guards were stretched out on the ground.

The cook stepped out of his shack. When he focused in on the two guards being dragged unconscious into the bunkhouse, he smiled and started to let out a shout of joy. Quickly he looked toward the mine and clamped his hand over his mouth. Elation was all over his face. He followed the procession into the bunkhouse.

The cook was a small man in his late sixties. He watched the two unconscious men being locked in the leg irons and chained to the metal beds. He eyed Keighley warily and said, "George, I thought you were—"

"I changed my mind," Keighley butted in.

"Hot diggity!" the old man shouted.

George introduced Clem Dobbins to Colt and Tanner. "Clem, you stay here and watch these two. If either of them starts to yell, mash 'em," Keighley said with a grin.

"Gladly!" Dobbins agreed. Keighley handed him one of the guards' guns.

"What time will they be coming out of the mine?" Dan asked Clem Dobbins.

"In about ten, fifteen minutes," Clem answered with a toothless smile.

The trio darted out the door and flattened their backs against the outside of the mine opening. Colt was on the left, guns in hands. Keighley and Tanner waited on the right. No more than five minutes passed when all went quiet in the mine. Soon voices were heard faintly. Slowly they became louder and more distinct.

They were almost to the opening. Dan whispered, "Get ready. The guards will be last."

Presently worn and weary men, their clothing caked with dirt, emerged into the fading light. Flattened tight against the rock walls, the trio waited. When the twelfth prisoner appeared, Dan bent his knees and poised himself.

The guards. One. Two. Three.

"Drop those guns!" Dan shouted. Before the guards could react, they were at gunpoint. The dozen slaves stood spellbound, as if they could not believe their eyes. The shocked, disarmed guards were ushered toward the bunkhouse. Dan remained with the grimy group, to fill them in on the situation.

"Which one of you is Tom Dolan?" Dan asked.

"I'm Dolan." The man was about Lily's age, Dan noticed. Even through the dirt Dolan had fine features. There was no doubting he was little Danny's father. The resemblance was unmistakable.

"Bill Rice?" Dan queried.

"That's me." Rice was maybe four or five years older than Nellie, Dan judged. A rugged man. Handsome in a leathery sort of way.

Dan introduced himself and filled them in on his latest knowledge of the Dolans and Nellie Rice.

Over a meal cooked with special care by Clem Dobbins, Dan laid out the plans for the liberation of Welcome at dawn. George Keighley had ridden back to town, reporting that Jim Feldman was not feeling well and was staying at the camp for the night. He was. In chains.

In passing Dan told how he and Logan Tanner had rolled the boulder on the escape hatch. They had a good laugh over how funny it would have been if any of the guards had sensed trouble and bolted into the mine, expecting to get out by way of the shaft. It was the only one in the mine.

As the happy band of men dispersed to prepare sleeping accommodations, Dolan and Rice lingered with Dan for more details. Bill Rice expressed concern that Nellie was at the hotel unprotected. Dan relieved his fears somewhat when he told him of Annie Rankin and Flora Bailey.

Tom Dolan's brow furrowed as Dan related how Mel Curry had slapped Lily, then eaten his cigar for it. "He'll be back, Dan. I know Curry. I've sure got to get home tomorrow." Tears filled his eyes. He squeezed Dan's shoulder. "I sure thank you for looking out for them."

Dan smiled broadly. "You've got a fine little family there, Tom."

After the lanterns were blown out, Dan lay in the dark, planning for the dawn attack. George Keighley would have guns for the mine slaves stashed behind the outhouse where the wagon wheel hung.

The man with the sore ribs hoped that Welcome could be freed without anyone getting killed. But he doubted it.

CHAPTER NINETEEN

Dawn was barely a gray hint on the eastern horizon as the twelve freed slaves and Logan Tanner hovered in the shadows of the forest at the east side of Welcome. The mountain air was brisk.

Dan Colt was making his way among the buildings to the Fireside Hotel. Primary in the move to free Welcome was the safety of the hostages held in the abandoned hotel. The guard stationed here was under Waite's orders to kill the hostages immediately upon any outbreak of trouble.

Slowly in the dim light Dan approached the side door of the hotel. He rapped lightly and waited. He knew the hostages were tied up. The only person who could open the door was the guard. Waite used only one man here, because aside from the elderly Howard Bailey the hostages were always women and children.

There was no movement inside. Dan rapped again a little harder. A shuffling sound followed. The latch on the door clattered and it creaked open slightly. A husky voice said in a half-whisper, "Who is it?"

With a like sound Dan said, "Tate Landry. There's trouble. Don't wake them. Come out here so I can talk to you."

The door came open. Dan heard the man swear. As he stepped out, he said, "What kind of troub—" Dan's gun barrel slammed against his head. The man dropped like a dead tree in a hurricane.

Someone inside was stirring. Dan stepped inside,

fished in his shirt pocket, and struck a match. A teenage girl sat up from a mattress on the floor. Dan held the match close to his own face. "I'm a friend," he whispered. The girl was blond and pretty. The fear which he saw in her eyes at first vanished.

"You're Marshal Lewis," she said.

There was no time to explain. "You're tied?" Dan asked.

"Hands and feet," she answered.

"Just a minute." Dan struck another match. "Hold up your hands." As she complied, he studied the knot and doused the match. As he worked the rope loose in the dark, he said, "You untie the others and keep them here till someone comes and tells you it's safe. Okay? Don't unlock the door unless you know it's a friend."

"Yes, sir."

After untying the girl's ankles, Dan took both lengths of rope, along with a section of blanket that he ripped loose, and was gone. Outside he tied up the unconscious guard and gagged him with the piece of blanket. Then he carried him to the outhouse and deposited him inside.

Logan Tanner was positioned among the trees where he could see the outhouse. In the gathering light he saw Dan carry the man and dump him in the privy. Then Dan turned toward the trees and waved his hat.

One by one the men darted across the clearing and approached the outhouse. Behind it Dan found sufficient guns and ammunition wrapped in a piece of canvas. As he handed each man a gun, he said, "All the townsmen have a piece of white cloth pinned to their sleeves. Don't shoot *them*!"

The dozen men had been instructed to scatter themselves among the buildings and wait. They were to pitch in and help wherever needed.

As the eastern sky burst into flame, Dan observed

the townsmen in their assigned positions. He quickly made his way to the wagon wheel hanging behind the outhouse. He smiled as he heard a muffled sound and a scraping noise from inside.

Along Welcome's street carefully positioned men were watching the edge of the Fireside Hotel.

Suddenly *there it was!* The wagon wheel bounded across the street. Before it slammed against the boardwalk, Dan heard doors being kicked in and glass shattering. As he bounded across the street for the Empire Saloon, a shotgun roared in the lobby of the Mayflower. Two shots were heard at the rear of the Empire. Gunfire broke out at the south end of town. As he charged the Empire, one of the opaque glass windows was smashed from the inside. As the glass shattered, a gun belched orange flame. The bullet hummed past Dan's ear. He hit the boardwalk and rolled against the building as the gun roared again.

Shots reverberated from inside the Mayflower. There was a gun battle going on down at the Rockaway Saloon. Waite's men apparently had decided to shoot it out, even against the odds.

Dan wanted to get Kyle Waite, himself. He wondered if this was Waite firing from the Empire window. A barrage of shots came from across the street, breaking more windows and splintering wood. From his prostrate position Dan saw that Logan Tanner was behind a rain barrel, throwing lead into the Empire. The gun was spitting fire just above Dan's head.

Kyle Waite had found that the pain in his broken nose increased when he lay down. He decided to sit up all night in a rocking chair in his sleeping quarters. Tate Landry, Alfredo Saldivar, and a hard case named Hy Walker were enlisted by Waite to stay up and keep him company. From time to time each had dozed, but none had slept. Waite figured if he had to spend a sleepless, miserable night, so should they. Just at dawn Walker thought he heard a strange sound in the back of the building. Peering through the window, he saw only deep shadows. He was unaware that waiting behind the privy was one of the townsmen positioned there to keep Waite from escaping out the back way.

Next to the outhouse was a shed where Waite and Landry kept their horses. From time to time Walker had looked out the window as daylight progressed. Just as the sun had brightened the land fully, one of the horses nickered. As Walker looked out, he heard a shotgun roar somewhere. He saw a man pull his head back behind the privy. Knowing the wood was old and dry, Walker fired two shots right through the outhouse. The man keeled over and lay still. By this time Saldivar had run to the saloon at the front. Hearing gunshots from down the street, he knew they had an uprising on their hands. The saloon windows had opaque glass. Smashing a section with his gun barrel, he saw Dan Colt coming at a run across the street.

By this time Kyle Waite was on his feet. As he heard Saldivar open fire out front, he said, "Tate, go help him." Landry bolted from the room. "We gotta get out of here!" the big man said to Walker. "You come with me."

Swaying somewhat, Waite moved to the door. No one was in sight. "C'mon, Walker," Waite grunted, "you can use Landry's horse. We've got to get to the mine and recruit some help."

Saddling the horses quickly, Waite and Walker headed up the east slope toward the mine road at a full gallop. As they sped away from the town, the sound of the gunfire faded. Topping a ridge, they looked back. Four horsemen were on their trail, coming fast. Someone had spotted them leaving and had taken up pursuit.

Charging their galloping mounts through the

rock-walled opening to the mining camp, they aimed for the bunkhouse. Waite was yelling at the top of his lungs, in spite of the pain it produced. Dismounting, he cast a glance at the mine. All was still. Suddenly the bunkhouse door opened and Clem Dobbins appeared, gun in hand. A voice from inside bellowed, "Boss! Help! We're all chained up!"

Walker fanned leather and fired, but Dobbins was just slamming the door. The sound of thundering hoofs on the trail behind them was getting louder.

"C'mon," said Waite. Between the bunkhouse and the mine opening was the supply shack. Walker was amazed at the strength Kyle Waite was exhibiting. He followed the swarthy man into the shack. Waite fumbled nervously, overturning boxes. He ran his hand into a wooden crate and produced four sticks of dynamite, fuses dangling. Checking his shirt pocket for matches, he dashed out the door.

Walker ran alongside Waite as he headed for the mine. "What are you going to do?" he asked breathlessly.

"We can't stand 'em off. There'll be more behind them. There's an escape shaft in the back of the mine. We'll collapse the opening so they can't follow. By the time they figure that we had a way out and *find* it, we'll be long gone."

Entering the yawning hole in the mountainside, Kyle Waite jammed the dynamite sticks in the cracks, two on each side of the opening. As he lit the first fuse, he said, "Head on back. We'll have about twenty seconds. Stay close to me. I know this hole like the back of my hand."

Just as Waite touched fire to the fourth fuse, the four horsemen charged through the opening. They saw Waite step into the darkness. Pulling their horses to a halt, they started to dismount. One of them heard the quadruple hissing of the fuses. Little puffs of smoke were lifting skyward.

"Dynamite!"

All four horses did a one-hundred-and-eighty-degree turn. Fast. The first stick boomed. The other three seemed to go all together. The earth shook as tons of rock thundered into the opening. Dust formed in great clouds. And suddenly all was quiet.

Remembering the shots from the back of the Empire, Dan motioned for Tanner to head back there. Another window was shattered from the inside. A second gun opened fire. Tanner, about to run toward the back, ducked down. From low level he peered at Dan, who had pulled his other Colt. One was aimed at one broken window. The second at the other. Tanner nodded that he understood. Dan cut loose, firing at both windows. Tanner bolted to the back of the building. The back door stood open. Expecting someone to come charging through the door, he ran into the empty horse shed. Some missing boards afforded a perfect view of the door, which moved slightly in the breeze.

Logan Tanner hung the barrel of his revolver over a board, sighted on the door, and waited. The smell of fresh horse droppings and the back door swinging loosely told Tanner that someone had already escaped.

Inside the Empire Landry and Saldivar jumped back as the fusillade ripped and tore through both windows. Landry said, "You stay here. I'll check on Waite." Saldivar was thumbing fresh shells into his pistol as Kyle Waite's hired gunslinger dashed to the back room.

Tate Landry cursed. He shouted to the Mexican, "Saldivar! That big ape and Walker have hightailed it!" Hearing Landry's shout, Logan Tanner opened fire, splintering the swinging door.

Again bullets were coming from below the window out front, shattering glass everywhere. Saldivar ran to the back. Landry was crouched low. Another shot made splinters scatter from the back door. "Get down!" shouted Landry.

While the two outlaws were agreeing that they must protect both front and back sides, Dan noticed four of the townsmen heading in a dead run for the livery stable. He thumbed fresh loads into both .45s and eased his way up the wall, adjacent to the broken window at the far end. Chancing a quick look, he saw that the gunmen had retreated to the back room.

Gunfire was still filling the air down the street. Dan knew Logan Tanner had the back door covered. Shouting through the broken window, Dan said, "Give it up, Waite! You're surrounded! You and whoever else is in there, throw out your guns and come out!"

"Waite's gone!" a voice retorted, followed by a laugh. "You'll never see him again!" Dan recognized Saldivar's accent.

"Give it up while you're still alive, Mex!" Dan shouted.

"Come in and get us!" Saldivar sprang to the inner doorway and fired six shots in rapid succession. Dan swung back as the bullets splintered wood and loosened shards in the broken window. In a fit of temper Saldivar shrieked, "Come on! Come in and get us!"

Another shot pierced the back door.

Landry snapped at Saldivar. "Get ahold of yourself, Saldivar! You just wasted six bullets."

The Mexican reached to his gunbelt. There were no more shells.

"Give me some of yours," he said to Landry.

"Not on your life, mister," the gunslick snapped. "There's a shotgun in the corner. Use it."

Saldivar picked up the double-barreled twelve gauge. Breaking it, he found it was loaded. Snapping it back, he started looking for extra shells. Several moments had passed since the last shot from Colt. They could still hear the fighting going on down the street.

Suddenly Dan Colt's voice came loud from out front. "Saldivar! I'm coming in!"

The Mexican crawled to the door which led into the abandoned saloon. Peering around the edge, he scanned the broken windows. His gaze lined on the front doors. Through the opaque glass he saw the tall form, Stetson and all, outlined clearly.

Saldivar looked across the floor to Tate Landry. "He's standing right outside the front doors," he whispered.

"Kill him!" Landry hissed.

Thumbing back both hammers, the Mexican stood up, ran through the door, aimed, and pulled both triggers. The shotgun roared. Both charges tore through the obscure glass, and the tall figure went down. A Colt .45 edged around the broken window at the far end and roared. Saldivar took the bullet at the base of his throat. He dropped in a lifeless heap.

As Tate Landry was calling the Mexican's name from the back room, Dan Colt picked up his hat and dusted it off. The cigar-store Indian lying on the boardwalk had two massive holes in its wooden chest.

"Sorry, Chief," said Dan, "but better you than me."

Landry bellied down and crawled through the doorway. "Saldivar," he called. "Saldivar!" The Mexican was lying dead with blood oozing from the hole in his throat. Landry took one look and headed for the back room. Just as he crawled through the doorway, the back door flew open from a hard kick. Logan Tanner came through, gun ready. It took him one second too long to spy Landry on the floor in the doorway. The outlaw's gun roared, and Tanner felt a bolt of fire sear his left thigh. The impact threw him through the door.

Landry sprang to his feet and lunged outside. Tanner was lying on his back in the mud. His gun lay six inches from his hand. Landry kicked the gun away. Blood was spreading over the fallen lawman's pant leg.

Landry stood over him, his eyes wild and threatening. He pointed his revolver between Tanner's eyes. Tanner was breathing heavily, holding his wound. The gunshots down the street were subsiding.

Thumbing back the hammer, the outlaw held it steady. "Call your friend back here, Marshal. Tell him you got me."

"That'd be cold-blooded murder, Landry," Tanner said grimly.

"Not if he uses his head. Me and him's gonna have us a little quick-draw contest." Gritting his teeth, he said, "You call him right now, or you're a dead lawman."

Tanner took a deep breath. Grimacing, he shouted, "Dan! Come out back! *I got Landry!*" Setting his eyes on Landry, he said, "You gunslicks just can't rest when you meet a man you have to test, can you?"

"Shut up," the outlaw hissed, glancing at the corner of the building.

"I told you, Tate. He's quick and he's deadly. He'll kill you."

As Tanner spoke, Dan Colt appeared at the corner of the building, guns holstered. He stopped abruptly, and his hands dropped toward the twin Colts.

Landry still held the muzzle between Tanner's eyes. "Hold it!" Landry shouted. Dan checked his hands. "We're gonna find out which one of us is fastest, Colt . . . Sundeen . . . or whoever you are. If you're willing to square off with me, I'll holster my gun, and your lawman friend can crawl out of the way."

It was then that Dan noticed Tanner's bleeding leg. "Is it bad, Tanner?" he asked.

"Bullet went through," the marshal told Dan Colt.

"Cut up some meat, but didn't hit the bone. Bleeding pretty bad."

Dan nodded. "Can you move out of the line of fire?"

Without answering Tanner began moving himself toward the building with his elbows.

Tate Landry set his eyes on Dan Colt and squared his shoulders. His face was fixed in stubborn lines.

Suddenly the firing down the street stopped. The town was abruptly silent. It was a silence that seemed to be permeated with death.

Dan Colt stood ready, hands poised over the handles of his guns. His ice-blue eyes were expressionless. His lips were tight against his teeth. "Make your play," he said evenly.

Logan Tanner pulled himself upward and leaned against the building. Neither man noticed.

Landry's hand darted downward. He felt the gun clear the holster just before both bullets ripped into his chest. The impact lifted him from his feet and flopped him on his back. He was still breathing as Logan Tanner stood over him, favoring the wounded leg.

The fallen gunfighter focused on Tanner's face as Dan Colt drew into sight. The smell of burnt gunpowder clung to the air. Landry looked at Tanner. His lips quivered. "Y-you're right." He swallowed hard. "He's all of it. *Quick . . . and deadly.*"

Dan slipped the .45s into their holsters. "Too bad it has to be Monday," he said sadly.

Tanner twisted his face. "Huh?"

"He told me of all the days to die, he thought Sunday was the nicest."

CHAPTER TWENTY

The citizens of Welcome gathered in front of the Mayflower Hotel as the sun reached its zenith in the azure Colorado sky. Dan Colt and Tom Dolan had saddled two horses and were preparing to leave.

The boardwalk across the street was lined with eleven corpses. Eight were Kyle Waite's men. Three were townsmen who died in the gun battle. The jail was cramped with the remaining gang members. Some were wounded.

Marshal Logan Tanner was bedded down in room number one in the Mayflower, under the care of Flora Bailey. Her husband watched the lady's nimble hands as she bandaged the wound. Two townsmen were also in the hotel, having their wounds treated. A couple of Welcome's teenage citizens were riding to Ouray to bring back the doctor and the sheriff.

Dan Colt turned to George Keighley. "George, I told you that you could ride out. You'd better get going before the sheriff arrives."

Keighley looked the tall man in the eye and said, "Ain't goin', Dan."

Before Dan's lips could form the question, Ed Sorenson spoke up. "We've already hired Mister Keighley as town marshal, Colt. He's one of us now."

A broad smile exposed Dan Colt's even white teeth. He gripped Keighley's hand. "Congratulations, Marshal."

"It's a straight line from here on, Dan," Keighley said with a note of self-assurance.

"You will see to the burial of the eight gang members?" Dan asked.

"Sure will," Keighley said, nodding. "One thing about Waite, Dan ..."

"Yeah?"

"I won't have to bury him."

Dan rubbed his nose and grinned slyly. "Nope. He took care of that himself."

"Well you know," said Keighley, "he wanted that mine more than anything in the world."

"Mm-hmm."

"He's got it all now. The *whole thing*."

The two men grinned at each other. Dan reached in his shirt pocket and handed Keighley a folded slip of paper. "Since you're marshal here, would you deliver this note to Tanner for me?"

"Sure."

They shook hands again. Dan told Ed Sorenson good-bye, then repeated the same to Annie Rankin. Bill and Nellie Rice stood next to Dan's horse, arms about each other. As Dan moved toward the horse, he saw tears on Nellie's cheeks. Bill extended his hand. Dan met it firmly. "Thank you, Mr. Colt," he said with emotion.

"Mr. Colt was my dad, Bill," Dan said, smiling. "I'm *Dan* to you." Looking at both of them, he asked, "You'll be riding home today?"

"We'll be leaving in about an hour," Rice answered.

Nellie stepped toward the tall man and reached upward. Dan lowered his head, and she planted a kiss on his cheek. "Please come back someday and see us."

Dan nodded. "Someday." Swinging into the saddle, he said, "Let's go, Tom. Lily's waiting."

"Tell Lily I'll be over in a day or two, Tom," said Nellie.

George Keighley stood on the front porch of the Mayflower and watched the two riders until they passed from sight at the edge of town. Swallowing a hot lump, he entered the hotel and ascended the stairs.

Logan Tanner was resting comfortably. He looked up at Keighley as the stout man entered the room. The Baileys were sitting next to each other, holding hands.

Tanner's husky voice broke the silence. "I understand they've made you marshal here, George."

"Yep," Keighley said, rubbing the badge with his sleeve.

"I want you to lock up Sundeen. Keep him in jail till I can ride."

"I never met Dave Sundeen, sir," Keighley said emphatically, "but Dan Colt is already gone."

Tanner's face reddened. "*Gone?*"

"Yep. Gone. But he left you this note," said Welcome's new marshal with a furtive grin.

Logan Tanner snatched the folded paper from Keighley's fingers. Keighley headed for the door. Pausing momentarily, he said, "Let me know if you need anything."

Tanner flashed him a look of disgust. Keighley disappeared, and the big man's thick fingers unfolded the note.

Tanner—
Sorry to leave you lying up there with a hole in your leg. But if I had not come running this morning when you hollered, you'd have one in your head. I cannot allow you to take me in. I must find my outlaw twin and prove that he exists, which will also clear me of all charges.
See you when I can bring Dave with me.
                                    Dan Colt
P.S. When you hollered for me this morning, you called me "Dan."

The sun was lowering toward the mountains as Dan Colt and Tom Dolan neared the last bend in the road before the Dolan ranch would be visible. Dan had filled in all the details for Dolan, concerning his false arrest in Holbrook, the five months in Yuma prison, and his search for Dave Sundeen.

As they rounded the bend, Dolan gasped. Dan focused on the shambled porch, the collapsed buildings, and the battered remains of the corral fence. Both horses were goaded into a full gallop. As they bounded over the bridge, the kitchen door opened and Lily came running through a path she had cleared in the debris. Tom's horse skidded to a stop. He was out of the saddle and had Lily in his arms before Dan could dismount.

Tom held Lily as she sobbed uncontrollably. Patty Ruth appeared in the door and stumbled twice before she reached her father. Dan waited patiently in the background.

After several moments of embracing her father the little girl ran to Dan. He picked her up and squeezed her good. As Lily composed herself, Tom said, "Where's Danny?"

"He's in the house," Lily answered with a touch of apprehension.

Tom sensed it immediately. "Is he hurt?" His eyes were raking over the thousands of hoofprints in the mud.

"Banged up a little, but he's all right," she said, trying to smile. Turning to the tall man, Lily said with feeling, "Dan, how can we ever repay you for bringing Tom back to us?"

"I've had enough pay already, just seeing you two together," he answered with a big smile.

"Lily, what happened?" Tom asked as they walked toward the house.

"Stampede," she said bitterly. "Curry's cattle. Yesterday." Lily paused at the door. She turned and her eyes met Dan's. *"Charlie's dead."*

Dan felt a bolt of heat flash through him. His mouth went dry. "How?"

Pointing to the path the cattle had taken from Curry's place on the west, Lily said, "Charlie was in the barn feeding the horses. Danny had gone with him and was playing by the water trough. When the cattle came, there was no way I could get to Danny. He saw them coming and was so scared he couldn't move."

Lily's lips were trembling. Tears filled her eyes. "I screamed at Danny. Charlie came out of the barn and saw the cattle bearing down on him. He ran into the path of the stampede and put Danny in the trough."

She looked at her husband. "That dear man saved our son's life, Tom." Turning her eyes on Dan, she blurted, "He knew it meant his own life, but he gave it for Danny."

A hot surge of fury was slowly bringing Dan Colt's blood to the boiling point. "Let's take a look at Danny," he said.

As they moved into the house, Dan said, "Tom, that stampede was no accident."

Dolan nodded. "I told you Curry would be back. I had no idea it would be like this."

Danny Dolan was asleep on the couch. The rays of the western sun cast a slanted pattern of yellow and orange shafts through the window. Tom examined the bruises on the boy's face and head.

"He must have raised up in the trough a time or two and the cattle bumped him," Lily said advisedly.

"He's been awake since?" Tom asked.

"Oh, yes. He's all right." Lily's eyes fastened on Tom's face, searching. "Now tell me. What happened at Welcome? Is Bill all right? What—"

Dan had wheeled and was storming toward the

door. "Dan! Where are you going?" Lily asked with alarm.

Dan Colt's mind was like an angry beast in a trap. He stopped at the door. When he turned, his face was a crimson mask of wrath. "I told Curry if he bothered you again, I would hunt him down like a cur dog. I aim to keep my promise. He could have killed Danny too." He stepped out the door, then stuck his head back in. "Where's Charlie's body?"

"In the barn," Lily answered, approaching the door. Tom moved beside her. "I haven't had the strength to dig a grave."

"I'll take care of it when I come back."

Tom stepped outside as Dan ran to the horse. "Dan, let me go with you!"

"You stay with Lily and the kids. This is something I want to handle myself."

Dan knew the quickest route to Mel Curry's house would be the same route the cattle took. He raked the bay gelding's sides. The startled animal bolted, and wind was immediately in the angry man's face.

The fence was still down where the cattle had come through. Dan thundered past the broken fence posts and gnarled barbed wire. The path of the stampede was easy to follow across the rolling pasture. It led straight to the main barn and corrals near the ranch house. Curry's men had started the stampede from there and guided the frightened beasts right through Dolan's place.

Dan was surprised to see no cattle or horses in the corral. The bunkhouse showed no activity. The place was like a graveyard.

Dismounting at the corral, he tied the sweating bay to a rail and pulled his right-hand gun. Curry would be expecting him. Cautiously he made his way toward the bunkhouse, watching every window. Kicking the door open, he waited for reaction. None came. The building was deserted. Except for some wadded bits of paper scattered on the floor and an old shirt hanging listlessly on a nail, the place was clean. The beds had been stripped of sheets and blankets.

Dan left the bunkhouse and walked a hundred yards to the house. He paused at the back door. "Curry! It's Dan Colt!" The evening breeze whipped around the eave of the house, making a soft moaning sound. The western sky was on fire, the clouds bursting into flame as the sun dipped behind the mountains.

Gun in hand, the tall man turned the knob and stepped into the kitchen. His gaze instantly fell on Mrs. Curry. She was seated at the table, her head flopped loosely on the top. There was a bullet hole in the back of her head. Dan judged by the dried blood she had been dead at least a full day.

There was a large sheet of paper lying on the table. It was a note, written in haste by Mel Curry. Dan carried it to the door and angled it toward the light of the sunset.

> To whoever finds this:
> I killed Tom Dolan and his little boy today. Didn't mean it that way, but I'm responsible. All my men quit and left. Cattle gone. Bessie. She turned against me too. Had to kill her. There's nothing to live for. Gunslick after me. Said he'd come like I was a cur dog. Can't stand it. Please give my ranch to Lily Dolan. Lily forgive me. Tom forgive me. Boy forgive me. Bessie forgive me. God forgive me. Cottonwood tree.
>
> Melvin Curry

Dan stepped outside. Scanning the scene, he saw a hill about a quarter of a mile south of the barn. At the crest of the hill stood a lone cottonwood.

Reining the bay to a halt at the crest of the hill, Dan saw the limp body of Mel Curry hanging at the end of a taut rope. The body moved slightly in the breeze. At the base of the hill stood Curry's saddled horse. The dead man's face was pointed directly east. Dan lifted his eyes in that direction. In the fading light he could see Tom Dolan's place, resting quietly in the valley.

"Take a good look, Curry," said Dan. "You wanted Tom's place. Take a *long* look. Was it worth all of this?"

By midday on Tuesday Dan Colt and Tom Dolan had buried the Currys side by side beneath the cottonwood tree.

After Dan had buried the gallant shotgunner at a spot near the river in the forest, the Dolans gathered around the grave for a brief service. The tall blue-eyed man fought tears while Tom Dolan read from the Bible.

The sun was setting on the western mountains when the black gelding felt Dan's weight settle on its back. It felt good to Dan to be on his own horse again.

"Sure wish you'd wait till morning to light out, Dan," Tom Dolan said warmly.

"I'll be in Ouray before midnight," he said, smiling. "I don't mind riding in the dark. My brother is out there somewhere. The quicker I get going, the quicker I'll find him."

Patty Ruth was mopping tears.

"When I grow up, I'm gonna be just like you!" Danny exclaimed with increased admiration.

The tall man smiled.

"You come back and see us," Tom urged.

"Someday," said Dan.

Lily Dolan could not speak. Through a thin wall of tears she watched the broad back of the tall man fading away. As the shadows swallowed him at the bend of the road, Lily found her voice and said, "Tom, do you think he will ever find his brother?"

Tom Dolan wrapped a strong arm about Lily's shoulder and cast a final glance at the spot where Dan Colt had last been seen. "Someday."

The long, shadowed twilight descended across the valley, lending its softness to the swaying trees, its touch of magic to the jagged profiles of the towering mountains. Darkness seemed to hesitate a little longer than usual. Then night settled its blissful peace over the valley.

Dell Bestsellers

- [ ] **SHOGUN** by James Clavell $3.50 (17800-2)
- [ ] **JUST ABOVE MY HEAD**
  by James Baldwin $3.50 (14777-8)
- [ ] **FIREBRAND'S WOMAN**
  by Vanessa Royall $2.95 (12597-9)
- [ ] **THE ESTABLISHMENT** by Howard Fast $3.25 (12296-1)
- [ ] **LOVING** by Danielle Steel $2.75 (14684-4)
- [ ] **THE TOP OF THE HILL** by Irwin Shaw $2.95 (18976-4)
- [ ] **JAILBIRD** by Kurt Vonnegut $3.25 (15447-2)
- [ ] **THE ENGLISH HEIRESS**
  by Roberta Gellis $2.50 (12141-8)
- [ ] **EFFIGIES** by William K. Wells $2.95 (12245-7)
- [ ] **FRENCHMAN'S MISTRESS**
  by Irene Michaels $2.75 (12545-6)
- [ ] **ALL WE KNOW OF HEAVEN**
  by Dore Mullen $2.50 (10178-6)
- [ ] **THE POWERS THAT BE**
  by David Halberstam $3.50 (16997-6)
- [ ] **THE LURE** by Felice Picano $2.75 (15081-7)
- [ ] **THE SETTLERS**
  by William Stuart Long $2.95 (15923-7)
- [ ] **CLASS REUNION** by Rona Jaffe $2.75 (11408-X)
- [ ] **TAI-PAN** by James Clavell $3.25 (18462-2)
- [ ] **KING RAT** by James Clavell $2.50 (14546-5)
- [ ] **RICH MAN, POOR MAN** by Irwin Shaw $2.95 (17424-4)
- [ ] **THE IMMIGRANTS** by Howard Fast $3.25 (14175-3)
- [ ] **TO LOVE AGAIN** by Danielle Steel $2.50 (18631-5)

At your local bookstore or use this handy coupon for ordering:

DELL BOOKS
P.O. BOX 1000, PINEBROOK, N.J. 07058

Please send me the books I have checked above. I am enclosing $_____
(please add 75¢ per copy to cover postage and handling). Send check or money order—no cash or C.O.D.'s. Please allow up to 6 weeks for shipment.

Mr/Mrs/Miss _____

Address _____

City _____ State/Zip _____

Another bestseller from the world's master storyteller

The Top of the Hill

IRWIN SHAW

author of *Rich Man, Poor Man* and *Beggarman, Thief*

He feared nothing... wanted everything. Every thrill. Every danger. Every woman.

"Pure entertainment. Full of excitement."—*N.Y. Daily News*

"You can taste the stale air in the office and the frostbite on your fingertips, smell the wood in his fireplace and the perfume scent behind his mistresses' ears."—*Houston Chronicle*

A Dell Book $2.95 (18976-4)

At your local bookstore or use this handy coupon for ordering:

| **Dell** | **DELL BOOKS** THE TOP OF THE HILL $2.95 (18976-4)
P.O. BOX 1000, PINEBROOK, N.J. 07058 |

Please send me the above title. I am enclosing $_____
(please add 75¢ per copy to cover postage and handling). Send check or money order—no cash or C.O.D.'s. Please allow up to 8 weeks for shipment.

Mr/Mrs/Miss_____

Address_____

City_____ State/Zip_____

AN OCCULT NOVEL OF UNSURPASSED TERROR

EFFIGIES

BY William K. Wells

Holland County was an oasis of peace and beauty...

until beautiful Nicole Bannister got a horrible package that triggered a nightmare,

until little Leslie Bannister's invisible playmate vanished and Elvida took her place,

until Estelle Dixon's Ouija board spelled out the message: I AM COMING—SOON.

A menacing pall settled over the gracious houses and rank decay took hold of the lush woodlands. Hell had come to Holland County —to stay.

A Dell Book $2.95 (12245-7)

At your local bookstore or use this handy coupon for ordering:

| Dell | DELL BOOKS
P.O. BOX 1000, PINEBROOK, N.J. 07058 | EFFIGIES $2.95 (12245-7) |

Please send me the above title. I am enclosing $ _____
(please add 75¢ per copy to cover postage and handling). Send check or money order—no cash or C.O.D.'s. Please allow up to 8 weeks for shipment.

Mr/Mrs/Miss_____

Address_____

City_____ State/Zip_____